THE
SOUL SEEKER:

A Deserved Death

R.R. Brikho

THE SOUL SEEKER: A DESERVED DEATH

Second Edition

Editor: Grace Fabbri

Cover Artist: Ken Krekeler

First Paperback Edition: June 2024

ISBN: 979-8-218-42144-1

Printed by IngramSpark in the USA

Published by Ambition Publishing LLC

www.ambition.pub

To my unwavering dedication toward bringing about the

world younger me had dreamt of for solace.

Table of Contents

CHAPTER 1 1

CHAPTER 2 13

CHAPTER 3 28

CHAPTER 4 42

CHAPTER 5 54

CHAPTER 6 66

CHAPTER 7 78

CHAPTER 8 90

CHAPTER 9 100

CHAPTER 10 111

CHAPTER 11 122

CHAPTER 12 137

CHAPTER 13 148

CHAPTER 14 160

CHAPTER 15 173

CHAPTER 16 185

CHAPTER 17 196

CHAPTER 18 207

CHAPTER 19 219

CHAPTER 20..232

CHAPTER 21..244

CHAPTER 22..256

CHAPTER 23..274

CHAPTER 24..286

CHAPTER 1

"I am a tool."

This was muttered ad nauseam from the lips of Tarias. He said this same phrase every night and morning. It was a comforting phrase. It disassociated his mind from what his hands had done. He was a tool. His actions were not his, for they were the will of a greater.

He never looked in the mirror. He did not care for his appearance. He told himself this as well. In fact, he feared his appearance, but this fear was struck down by his repetitive phrase.

"I am a tool."

A tool did not have feelings. A tool did a job, and it did not moan or whine. It just did what it was meant to do.

Tarias stood up from a straw bed. The room he was stored in was small. A tool did not need much space. He dragged himself over to the wall where a cloak hung. It was gray and had been made to cover the entire body, protecting it from view. His beige hands grabbed the cloak from the wall and wrapped it around his body, and he stepped his callused feet out of his room.

He was allowed to keep his face uncovered in this town, for this was a town in his homeland of Teruk. It wasn't like many of his fellow people cared to look at him. He was unimportant. He was born to no name. Some avoided him, for his skin was slightly beiger than it was tan. Terukians were a strict people—they did not deviate from the mores and laws of their society, for to do so would bring about an appropriately strict punishment.

The streets of Aigerua were filled with people with jagged ears, and, when looking at the mass of heads in the crowd, they resembled a field of long grass. The streets were lined with finely pruned trees. Their leaves were green, and in between these trees were fountains that spouted water into a small watering ditch that ran along the edge of the tan brick roads. Azkozals, feathered horse-like creatures with beaks, could often be seen getting a drink in these watering ditches next to their masters.

Tarias walked on, surrounded by fellow Terukians. The streets were rarely ever clear of people. He reached a small building down the road. This building looked like any other building in Aigerua. It was made of brown stone bricks with green-painted log posts that propped up an overhang surrounding the building. Tarias walked to the door of the building and knocked on it.

An elfe opened the door. Tarias's eyes met hers, but he quickly set them downcast. This elfe was beautiful, but she was a Midlandesq elfe. It was not proper for a Sealandesq elf to enjoy the beauty of a Midlandesq elfe, and it was surely wicked for a tool such as Tarias to do so. She stepped aside, pointing into the room. Tarias went where she had pointed.

There was a small square tile rested atop the carpeted floor. Tarias knelt on it, and its hard surface ached his knees. A door creaked open, and Tarias could hear the sound of footsteps crossing the room. When they came to a stop, he could only see a pair of boots, well-stitched and made of dark leather.

"Raise your head, soul seeker," said an elf's voice.

Tarias lifted his head. The elf stared down at Tarias. He wore a green tunic with a lamellar armor covering it, and a mask that covered his whole face. The mask was black, and it had jagged teeth with eyebrows that slashed downward angrily. It had pointy ears, but unlike those of a Terukian, they aggressively jutted upwards. The handle of a sword hung on his waist. It did not have a blade. It was only a handle.

"You are to kill an elfe tonight. She will be in attendance at the feast at the Palace of Aigerua. Make it a quiet death. I do not wish for suspicion that it was an assassination. It should look natural."

Tarias looked up. "Would it aid me if I had her name?"

"No. She will be wearing green. She will be adorned with golden cuff bracelets, and every elf present at the feast will be fawning over her. She also has a tattoo of an azkozal skull on her back, at the base of her neck."

The masked elf pulled out a sheet of paper and presented it to Tarias. It had a drawing of an azkozal skull on it.

"That is enough information for you to get the job done."

Tarias nodded his head. He never asked why he was to kill. He just kept his mouth shut and did as he was told. He was a tool. The black-masked elf ordered Tarias to stand, so he did. The elf walked into another room and came back out with a scroll in his hands. He unraveled the scroll and began to read.

"Due to your unwavering dedication, His Imperial Majesty, long may he live, has set aside this building for you to use. This arrangement will be finalized once you complete this mission. It comes with everything that is currently stored within, as well as the servant elfe that tends its grounds."

Tarias's eyes went wide and shot over to look at the elfe. He shook his head and turned his eyes back to the ground. His face quivered, and he struggled to react with grace.

"Is there something wrong, Tarias?"

Tarias shook his head. "No, of course not. I am grateful."

"Wonderful," said the elf. "You may leave."

Tarias turned around and exited the building. He went straight for the road. Sometimes, when he roamed the streets, the Midlandesq Terukians would try to walk through him. It was a joke to move out of the way for a Sealandesq elf. Tarias stepped out of their way. It was the right thing to do. It was what he was supposed to do.

The sight of the Terukian Palace of Aigerua was an unavoidable one. It dominated Aigerua's skyline, and its towering green walls could be seen from anywhere in town. The walls were almost excessively tall, like they were made to affirm that outsiders were not meant to be inside. Only the tips of the buildings within could be seen behind them, and green and gold gargoyles perched themselves on the edges of their roofs.

Tarias marched over to the palace. Upon his arrival, he noticed a group of Terukian elves praying at the base of the wall. Kneeling before it, they looked like ants. He knew that it would have been foolish to try and scale such a wall with no footholds, so he kept walking, circling the building in search of a new way in.

He watched the soldiers patrol around the walls for hours. As he expected, there were no holes in their sightlines. Tarias did not allow himself to become frustrated, for he had expected this from the guards of the Palace. There were, undoubtedly, other soul seekers within their ranks. Only the best were kept to guard the Emperor's family, and Tarias knew it would be foolish to pick a fight with any of them. They wore the same green color as the Emperor. It was the same shade that Tarias's superior wore, as well.

Calmly, Tarias kept walking. He knew that if there were other soul seekers about, then they would be watching the crowds surrounding the Palace for any suspicious behavior. It was too early to enter the Palace. Knowing this, Tarias left the area and headed towards one of the local bathhouses to clear his mind and dwell on his strategy.

Tarias would frequent bathhouses often. In truth, it would be strange for a Terukian *not* to frequent a bathhouse. They were a means to cleanse both the body and the mind, and it was not uncommon to see people from all walks of life in a public bathhouse. Merchants, laborers, warriors, and monks all frequented them.

Tarias bathed himself before every infiltration, for he did not wish to smell foul. He scrubbed the dirt from his hands and feet with herbal soaps. Stories of other soul seekers being caught because of their lack of due diligence concerned Tarias. He thought of how much shame it would bring him to be caught due to the neglect of his hygiene. He made sure to take his time. Tarias made sure to always act as if there was always another soul seeker in the room looking for him; if he were to so hurriedly leave the bathhouse, it would have been a noticeable and strange behavior. Terukians basked in the bath waters. They did not rush out. So Tarias rested there until he almost fell asleep, which was often a tell that one had been in the bathhouse for a bit too long.

He exited the bathhouse, but he made sure to pilfer a pair of slippers before he left so that he could keep his clean feet from dirtying once more. The sun had already begun to lower from the top of the sky, but Tarias did not worry about his task. It would be completed. Tarias had never failed. He had other concerns, in any case—he was clean like a Midlandesq person, but he was not dressed like one, let alone dressed like someone that was to enter the Palace. His eyes hovered over the countless trade stalls that lined the roads. He did not carry money, because he had no use for it. What would be the use of keeping coin for an elf who could just steal whatever he wished without fear of being caught?

Tarias danced through the crowds of people. He slipped golden bracelets from the wrists of rich merchants, and he pulled an expensive black silk shawl from a lady in passing. Rarely did those he robbed notice that they had been thieved from, and even if they did, Tarias already slipped away into the crowd before he could be found. He stripped a dark green jant from a stall and slipped into an alleyway. He opened up the jant and placed the jewelry and shawl inside, hiding the garments underneath his gray robes.

Tarias ventured back to the palace and once more examined the scene around it. There was a group of individuals outside the palace that had not been present before. They wore the color orange, and they guarded a wagon. It must've been the elves of some Erdoark, or some other merchant visiting the Palace that evening. No matter who it was, they were going to be the soul seeker's door to the inside of the Palace.

He stalked the orange-dressed soldiers. They all wore similar lamellar armor, a normality of dress for Terukian soldiers, and they all stood at attention. They watched the crowds around them, and they were waiting. Tarias did not see their superior, but he assumed that, whoever he was, he was off enjoying the local sights of the capital, as rich visiting elves often did.

Tarias turned away from the Palace, and he sought the nearest brothel. His feet floated him through the crowds.

When he reached a building where a brown azkozal with an orange cloth draped over it for riding stood tied at a post, he laughed to himself—the behaviors of the powerful were so predictable.

He shook the thought away. He had a task, and it was improper to take his mind away from it. A guard stood near the azkozal and watched it. The brothel was next to an alleyway, but the guard was standing right at the entrance. Tarias continued to walk around in search of another entrance into the alleyway.

It was not long until he found another entrance. The guard's back was facing him, so Tarias grabbed a pebble and chucked it at him. The guard turned and spun around, reaching for the handle of his sword. Tarias could not see the elf's face, but he could imagine what he might've looked like underneath his helmet. The guard charged at Tarias, ready to beat him; however, once he came within arm's reach, Tarias slipped to the side and tripped the guard, wrapping his arm under the elf's shoulder. He stomped on the elf's sword hand and wrapped his arms around his neck. He squeezed and did not let go. The elf thrashed. His limbs flailed like an animal that was caught in a trap, but because Tarias did not release his hold, his limbs duly went limp. Even then, Tarias did not let go; he held on for another long moment to make sure the elf would not trouble him later.

Tarias undressed the elf. He put on the orange jant the guard had worn, as well as his lamellar armor and helmet. He hid the body in an uncovered sewer hole, and he stored his gray robes under a rock. He fastened the guard's sword to his hip while he walked back to the azkozal. The guard's flailing had led to a bit of dirt tarnishing the armor, so Tarias reached down to the watering stream and scrubbed it off.

Soon enough, the superior that the guard was protecting left the brothel.

"Nagus Oridi, let us head back to the Palace. I have had my fun with the local wretches."

CHAPTER 2

Nagus Oridi was Tarias's new name; or, rather, it was his new name until his task was done. As he walked down the streets, he carried the lead of the azkozal and pondered on how he ought to conduct himself. The title of Nagus was an honorable one amongst levies, and he should at least hold himself to the same level of honor. Oridi was a very Southwestern name. The elf he killed was probably from around Mt. Kalarn, which stood near the Uhric Pass. The fact he was a Nagus eliminated the chance of his superior being a merchant, and there was only one aristocrat from that area who wore the color orange.

The elf he was now following was surely Yodoa: the Alboark of the Southwestern Sphere.

This was a pleasant stroke of luck for Tarias. Usually, he would have to work far harder to achieve success in his mission; but to be following this whoring Alboark, a powerful and lustful elf, on the task to assassinate an elfe hearing suitors was a blessing from the Emperor. It was an especially pleasant thought to Tarias that he would not have to kill any innocent people on the way to the target.

Tarias shook his head. *I am a tool,* he thought. *A tool does not have wants. A hammer does not care for the nail it strikes.*

"Nagus. Is your head alright?" asked Yodoa.

The Alboark must have noticed that Tarias was lost in thought. Tarias smiled, raised his left palm forward, and nodded his head to show that he was fine. Yodoa shook his head and continued forward. They returned to the armored elves who guarded the Alboark's wagon, and Tarias attached the azkozal to the front of the wagon to lead it. The Alboark led his elves, and his azkozal led the other bird mounts. Tarias had been a member of countless armies, so disciplined matters like this were second nature to him. Yet, never had he fought under his own name.

The gates began to lift from the ground. Soon, there was an entrance into the palace, and the elves began their march into the Palace of Aigerua. They passed through the gates, and Tarias's eyes wandered, but he kept his head forward. He was astonished at the Palace's beauty, but he knew it would be unwise of him to turn. The road inside the Palace was paved with white bricks with inscriptions exclaiming glory to the Emperor. At their perimeter were gold bricks that had old Terukian glyphs etched into them. There were several servants cleaning the roads or tending to the shrubbery that lined them, but they were dressed less like servants and more like monks. They wore white robes, and they treated the Palace grounds like they were a temple. Guards dressed in green jants and who wore full lamellar armor lined the roads. They did not move. They stood like statues anchored into the ground. They stood so still that Tarias would not have been surprised if their feet were nailed to the ground.

They traveled over a green wooden bridge that crossed over a small stream. This stream marked the entrance into the Palace gardens, and soon the elves were surrounded by trees, shrubs, flowers, and small critters. He could see the other elves looking around and gasping like they had not seen any of these things before, so Tarias feigned a similar reaction.

Past the garden was the Palace of Aigerua itself. To say it was large was an understatement. What it lacked in height it made up for in width. It spanned far past the limits of the eyes, and Tarias had to turn his head to take all of it in. An elf stood in front of its doors, and he wore a black mask and green jant.

It was Tarias's superior; rather, his true superior, waiting at the front for the Alboark to kneel. Yodoa did. He knelt immediately.

"I, Alboark Yodoa, beg entry into the Palace. I wish to feast with the Emperor, and I wish to praise his glory."

The black-masked elf nodded. He turned to the side and extended his arm to the Palace doors. Tarias squinted. *Strange.* Why would his superior be here? It was truly an odd situation.

Or maybe it was not—maybe Tarias ought not to question what his superior was doing here and instead ought to focus on his task. Yodoa ordered a few of his elves to take the wagon over to where the other wagons were parked in the courtyard, and he beckoned for 'Nagus Oridi' to follow him into the Palace.

Tarias nodded, and he followed the Alboark inside. Upon entrance, he could not keep himself from gazing in awe at the interior of the Palace. Trinkets made from korotuu, an overwhelmingly shiny metal, decorated the walls. So much korotuu in one area gave the air an energetic feel, and it hazed Tarias's mind. Thoughts came to him more quickly. He would hyperfocus on one thing, and within a second his attention would jump to something else. He shook his head, trying to clear the sensation from his mind.

Eventually, the feeling regulated. His mind had adjusted to the room, similar to how one's eyes would adjust to sudden darkness. Soon enough, everything came slower to his head, and he finally regained his ability to stay focused. Some of his counterparts did not react at all. The Alboark certainly had—

he gawked at the old carvings in the walls—but his elves did not question it. It seemed as if they were used to his reaction. Tarias thought it strange, but he continued on.

They passed through a final pair of doors, and they were greeted with the sight of the throne room. It was a square shape. On the border of the room was tile that was sectioned off from the center by gold columns. These gold columns had etchings that celebrated the Terukians, specifically the Midlandesq, and depicted their vast armies. Just past these columns was something incredibly strange. There was no sunlight in the throne room, but *grass* grew on the floor. The grass looked even greener, healthier, and better maintained than the grass outside. A path led to the throne of the Emperor. It was unlike any throne Tarias had seen before. It sat on a dirt mound, and atop the mound was a disc made of korotuu. The Emperor was not present, but an elfe dressed in green was. She stood lower on the mound, and she looked around at tables full of elves that sought her attention. These tables surrounded the mound on tiled sections of the floor below. There were no torches or chandeliers to brighten the room, but it certainly was not dark. The korotuu disk that stood on top of the mound reflected light all over the room, and to look at the disk itself would burn the eyes.

As she stood, she was effortlessly beautiful. She caught the elves' focus like a punch to the face. She had Tarias's focus as well, but he did not look at her with the wish to bed her. As they walked closer, Tarias and a few other elves were ordered to stay at the perimeter. Sealandesq folk were not allowed in the inner of the room, and none of the Erdoarks or Alboarks there had any guards at their side. The Arks became restless, and many of them started muttering menial things to one another. Soon after the mutterings started, two elves and a surplus of guards in green entered the throne room. The elfe in the green dress stepped lower down the mound, but she still kept in the center of it. The first elf stood behind the green-dressed elfe to her right. He waited halfway up the mound, and to keep his balance, his left leg was planted slightly higher than his right. He stood about half a head taller than the rest of the other Terukians in the room, and his black hair was grayed with age. His smile was barely noticeable, with just the edges of his lips raised. He too wore green, the color of Terukian royalty, and kept his arms crossed. The other elf looked nigh-identical to the first elf that walked in, but his body was decorated with gold cuffs, necklaces, earrings, and rings.

The Arks all wore crowns, and they were proud of them. Listening carefully, Tarias could hear them teasing each other: pointing out how poorly polished another Ark's crown was, or how few jewels he had. Afterward, they would point to their own crown and exclaim how superior it was. Tarias squinted his eyes at the Arks for their behavior, but he understood that it was in their nature as Midlandesq to do so.

The elf with gold cuffs did not wear a crown. He climbed to the top of the mound and stood on the disk. Upon contact, his skin began to glow slightly. Some parts of his skin shone brighter than the others, with markings seeming to draw in the light. Tarias tried to read them from afar, but his eyes did not have the capacity to do so. The elf sat cross-legged on the disk and closed his eyes.

The elf in the green jant and black mask walked to the mound and stood to the left of the elf.

"All hail the Emperor! The Koroark! The door to our people's past, and the key to our people's future! The closest to the heavens! All RISE!"

At once, everyone stood and faced the Koroark. They bowed their heads and raised their hands. A chant began, and they cried their love for the Emperor. Once they finished, they sat back down, and the black-masked elf stood forward.

"The Alboarks shall present their offers of marriage first, in the order of the Alboark from the northwesternmost territory to the Alboark of the southeasternmost territory. Then, it shall be the Erdoarks using the same order. And finally, it shall be whoever else with the pungent courage to make an offer to the princess with such a low status."

There were four Alboarks out of five present. They each presented lavish gifts and grand promises to the lady, but she seemed largely uninterested. Tarias's head spun with confusion. Two of the Alboarks were married with children, yet they ask for this elfe's hand in marriage? He didn't understand it.

Tarias shook his head again and reminded himself of his position.

Eventually, Yodoa came up to the Princess. He pulled a small black box from his side satchel. It looked to be made of a black stone, and when he opened it, it revealed a necklace that was glowing with a blinding white light. He held it up to the elfe and bowed his head.

"Even if you do not choose me, good princess, I ask that you accept my gracious gift. I will stand with you to the end, and it is my wish to stand side-by-side with your magnificence."

The lady in the green dress nodded her head to the black-masked elf. He walked to Yodoa, grabbed the korotuu necklace from him, and walked it back to the lady. She examined it with her hands. Once finished, she handed it back to the black-masked elf.

"I accept your gift, Alboark Yodoa," said the lady, with a voice softer than the pelt of a mink.

Yodoa smiled at the lady and bowed his head.

"Why do you think you are suited to be my consort?" she asked.

Yodoa stood up and puffed out his chest. "Princess Elreina, I am the most prestigious Alboark present. I control the lands near Mt. Kalarn, and I have had the most experience here in commanding elves. It is only appropriate to have a proper elf with proper experience leading the Terukian people."

Princess Elreina laughed. "Is that the last Alboark? Next suitor, please come up."

Yodoa turned his head and grimaced. He stomped over to his seat and leaned back with crossed arms. A dozen more suitors presented themselves to the Princess. She had a similar response to each of them: a general disinterest and an urge to get the event over with. Once the final suitor presented his case, plates of food were run out to the tables. The servants that brought them out wore green. Everyone wore green but the visitors. When the Princess left the room, the guests began to chow on the food presented to them, but Yodoa shook his head and stormed toward Tarias.

"Nagusi and the rest of you, follow me. I am sick of this event."

Tarias waited until the rest of the orange-clothed bodyguards had fallen into line behind the Alboark. He took a spot in the back of the group, and together they walked back to the wagon they'd dragged to the Palace. Yodoa leaned forward on it.

"Elves. We will rest here in the auxiliary barracks. Act with manners. You may go."

The elves bowed. Tarias began his march with his fellow elves. The auxiliary barracks were on the other side of the courtyard, and it took them only a short walk to reach it. There was no door to the barracks, only an empty archway, so the elves waltzed on in. Most of the beds inside were empty. Tarias assumed Yodoa's elves were the first to occupy them. He quickly chose a bed nearest to a window and laid one of his gauntlets on it to claim it for himself. The rest of the elves did the same, and then erupted into chatter.

Tarias did not want to be caught in conversation with the rest of these elves, as he did not know how close they were with the elf he was impersonating, so he immediately left the barracks. He heard calls for him, but he lifted a single finger, telling them he would take but a moment. He turned down a hallway and used his peripheral vision to peek into each room. About half of the doors were closed, but one had been left open. He entered one, keeping his head down when servants dressed in green came walking down the halls.

Tarias shut the door behind him, and he was met with a hole in the ground. It was a rectangular hole about as long as half of Tarias's leg and about as wide as his forearm. He removed the dead elf's helmet from his head and unclipped the armor. Immediately after, he disrobed, removing the orange jant and placing it on the ground next to the squat toilet. All that remained on him was the wrapped green jant that hid underneath his clothes. He placed this on the floor as well while he unwrapped the green jant, revealing the black shawl and jewelry that was wrapped inside. He began to place the items of jewelry on his person. Soon enough, his wrists were adorned with gold braces. Tarias needed to make sure to follow the customs of the guards of the Palace, for they all competed with each other when it came to wealth.

Tarias folded up the orange jant and dropped it into the squat toilet. It fell into a stream of water and was whisked off to a place only the muck scrapers knew. He wrapped his body with the green jant and covered his head with the black shawl. The helmets and lamellar coats that the Alboark's elves wore were just the same as any other elf's armor. They were all made the same, for every soldier was to be the same. The Emperor did not tolerate deviance, and when it came to other Terukians, the sentiment was shared. He clipped the armor back on, put on his boots, and covered his head with the helmet.

"Hello? Is there anyone in this room?"

Tarias turned his gaze to a stream of running water that was recessed into the ground at the end of the room. There was a metal ladle that sat on the floor next to it, and he hastily began to wet the squat toilet. He let out a sigh and ran to open the door.

It was just a servant lady. She was about a full head shorter than Tarias, and she peeked into the room behind him.

"Apologies, dear elfe. I have left a mess, and it would not have been right to leave it to another," said Tarias as he dropped to his knees and bowed.

"Ah, it looks rather clean. You have my thanks. You may rise, gentle elf," said the servant lady.

She had olive-tan skin, and Tarias had beige. Tarias left her with a smile, which was about as much as was allowed for a Sealandesq elf to give to a Midlandesq elfe. He hurried out of the restroom and went out to the courtyard. The sun was about three-quarters to the horizon at this point, and Tarias set his eyes upon the Palace.

CHAPTER 3

Tarias marched his way to the palace with the gait of a soldier following a command. He moved in a hurry, but he did not strut too fast. He did not wish to bring too much attention to himself. He watched the guards that stood outside the Palace. His heart pounded a bit. He did not want to be stopped; he could not afford to halt and hold a conversation with them. He kept walking, and the guards stood still. He could feel their gaze on him. He kept up his speed and soon made it to the entrance.

They did not stop Tarias. Tarias rushed inside and went to the throne room. All the Arks had finished the meals that were presented before them. Most of them were pudgy like

Yodoa, and their rolls rested on the tabletops they leaned on. The princess was still gone, and only the Koroark and the two elves who stood at his sides were present. Tarias's gaze was anchored on the Koroark, and he found himself lost in a daydream while he stared at him.

Has he sat in that same place for this long? Tarias asked himself.

The Koroark opened his eyes. His eyes *glowed*, and the sight of them made Tarias jump. The Koroark was certainly aware of Tarias's presence. He was aware of *everyone's* presence. Tarias had never questioned his superior's orders, but he suddenly wondered: why would the Koroark wish for his daughter to be killed? Why would he be delegated this job?

Tarias gritted his teeth. It felt like sandpaper on his molars. Sweat beaded down from his armpits, and he felt like he did not have enough air.

Stop it, Tarias. Stop it, his mind ordered him.

He closed his eyes and breathed in through his nose. He took several deep breaths, and his breaths forced a stretch in his diaphragm. He breathed out through his mouth, and soon, he calmed down. His eyes burst open with focus. He glanced over every Ark in the room. They were all reveling, unaware of the happenings outside the grassy floors of the throne room. Tarias crept around the room's perimeter. He passed by all the Ark's soldiers in their colorful jants, and he found himself walking down one of the side halls that split from the throne room. There were not many guards in these halls. Should the Palace of the Koroark not be filled to the brim with elves who worshipped him? Ought it not be the safest place for him? Tarias was concerned; the Emperor deserved many more elves to protect him. But the black-masked elf *did* stand next to him, and although he was not a soul seeker himself, he certainly had the skills to best Tarias.

Tarias turned a corner, and he saw the green-dressed Princess speaking to an elf. She was flanked by two guards, and she stood with her arms crossed, shaking her head. Tarias could feel her displeasure. The elf she spoke to shook his head and stormed away, so she turned around and entered the door behind her. Her elven guards stood with discipline in front of her shut door.

It would be stupid for Tarias to enter from the front. Far too many people were here for a quiet kill. But her door was not the only one that had lined the wall—he could sneak in through another room, he realized, and then climb around from the outside.

Thank the Koroark for windows, Tarias told himself.

He waited until the guards were sufficiently bored. As soon as they started to make small talk with each other, Tarias gingerly walked into the room across from him. In it, there was a large window that overlooked the gardens in the rear of the Palace. The sun was low in the sky.

He watched the people below. Again, there were not many of them. Tarias imagined most of the people were still inside the throne room. However, he still thought it safer to wait and lurk until there was no one left in the gardens. The Princess's room was two rooms down; or rather, two *windows* down. His armor was heavy, but he did not wish to leave it in this room. He reckoned he would have to suffer the climb to the next room fully armored. He shrugged—this was no issue—and he hid behind a curtain until the sun fell even lower.

Once the sun gently grazed the horizon, Tarias stretched his arms. He looked out of the window once more. There were still people outside, but the sky was now dark. Tarias climbed on the windowsill, and he gripped his fingers onto the stone bricks that made up the palace's exterior walls. His green jant blended him into the walls, and his fingertips pulled him to the next room. He peeked inside. No light shined through the curtains, and no breaths were heard. He jumped into the room. There was a drawbar on the door. Tarias rushed to it and placed the bar to lock the door.

Tarias shed the armor from his torso. He laughed to himself. He remembered that he left his other gauntlet on his bed in the barracks. He shed the right-hand gauntlet from himself as well, for he had no use for armor. He hid the helmet and the rest of the stolen armor inside a wardrobe. There were several jants and other items of clothing inside. When he looked up, he realized that the sky had grown even darker—he had to hurry into the next room.

He felt lighter now, and he glided across the outside walls of the Palace. He passed the next room, and he found himself hanging outside the window of the Princess's room. Flickering candlelight shined from it, but he could hear small puffs of breath—she was blowing the candles out. The light from the window grew darker.

Tarias pulled himself up, and he gently put his feet down onto the floor of the room. Princess Elreina stood with her back to Tarias. At the base of her neck was a tattoo of a bird skull—an *azkozal* skull. She held a candle in her hands and prepared to blow it out. With a quick puff of air, the room went dark.

"Who is that?" Elreina spun around to face the window.

Tarias's palm caught the exhale from Elreina's mouth. She went stiff like a board, and Tarias felt her hands scramble for his wrist. He grabbed the extinguished candle from her hand, placed it down, and squeezed his hand over her mouth. He wrapped his other arm under hers and held her nostrils closed. He could feel her attempt at life; she dug her teeth into his palm. He *squeezed* even more. He squeezed until she went limp. He walked backward and prepared to set her down on the ground. He knew she was not dead yet, only unconscious, and that he would have to continue to stop her from breathing. A glancing stare brushed over his bloodied palm. He knelt.

He fell to his knees. There was a small bump where her belly was. He shook his head.

"I am a tool," he whispered to himself, a blank expression on his face.

Her eyes opened. She gasped for air, and she clawed at Tarias's arms. He closed his eyes, not wanting to see what he was about to do, and grabbed a pillow that was on top of the Princess's bed. He pressed it onto her face and *pushed*. She tried to scream through it, but the pillow dampened her voice. She kept on clawing. For a long time, she would not stop; but soon, her clawing arms landed with a thud on the ground. Tarias still kept pressing.

He got back to his feet and walked toward the window, but he did not climb out. Instead, he sat on the windowsill and stared at the lifeless body of the Princess. His mind told him to flee immediately, but his feet felt like they were stuck in tar.

He stood there, frozen, until he heard on the door. Suddenly, reality struck him. He climbed up onto the windowsill and pulled himself down. He slowly descended from the room. He tried not to think of the task. The task was already done, and nothing could be done about it. He breathed in through his nose and out through his mouth. He wanted to calm his heart, for he knew soon the alarm bells would be ringing. He would have to run, and he felt more comfortable running when calm.

Just as his feet finally touched the ground, he heard yelling coming from above. He started running. He chose to cut through the grass of the gardens, and soon bells were ringing all around him. Torchlights were lit, and elves in armor ran around lighting every torch or firepit they could. Tarias kept to the darkest parts of the palace grounds, and he secured his black shawl over his face.

"You there! Halt!"

Whoever had called out to Tarias soon had their voice fade away into a murmur. Tarias was too fast for them, or he was at least faster than most of them. In his peripheral vision, an elf with a black mask, his *superior*, lingered on top of the Palace walls. The elf stared down at Tarias, motionless. Tarias picked up his speed. He was confused as to why his superior was watching him.

The elf dropped down from the walls and burst into a sprint toward Tarias. Tarias ran even faster. The gates were right in front of him, but to go that way would be a waste of time—he would never make it through them. His eyes wandered up the wall. There was nothing of use in front of him. He cursed, for he did not wish to overexert himself. He ran straight for the gate. There was no other option. He was going to have to run through it.

He felt his hand yanked. He turned around, and he saw the black mask. The Palace was not behind him, and when Tarias turned around, he did not see the gates. He was in an alleyway, and far behind the elf in the black mask were the green outer walls of the Palace of Aigerua.

"Why did you help me escape?" asked Tarias.

"It was necessary. I am impressed. This was not a suitable task for a lone soul seeker, yet you still delivered."

Tarias bowed. "Thank you, Master."

"Return to the building you met me in this morning. It is your new base of operations. I will inform you of your next task when I need you." The elf disappeared into a puff of black smoke.

Tarias set off to locate the rock he'd hidden his gray robes under. It was not a short walk, and Tarias naturally kept his head swiveling around out of fear of being watched. He lifted the stone and changed. He kept the green jant and black shawl with him, but he removed the gold bracelets from his arms and dropped them to the floor. He did not need them. What did a soul seeker need jewelry for? His status was not nobility, but a tool to be used.

He knocked on the door to the home. The servant elfe opened up, and Tarias immediately bowed.

She laughed. "No need, Master. You may rise."

Tarias paused. He was unsure of how to proceed. He was a Sealandesq elf. This was not normal. This was not typical. Why was this happening? Tarias closed his eyes and stood up. He shook his head.

"Are you alright, Master?" asked the elfe.

"I am fine. Thank you for your concern."

Tarias walked past the elfe. He took in the room once more. He hadn't thought much about it before, but now, since it was *his*, he figured it would be worth the time to get acquainted. There were plenty of golden knickknacks and embroidered furnishings. It looked to be the typical Midlandesq house, and Tarias grew ever more uncomfortable.

The fireplace was lit. He sat down on his heels on a mat in front of it. The green jant and black shawl were still in his hands. He tossed them both into the fire.

No evidence. No evidence, no getting caught.

He turned his head. The elfe servant stood in the corner with a smile. His eyes naturally looked her up and down. She was dressed in a gray silk dress. She had jewelry covering her thin arms, and they were pointing to an open door.

"Master, your room is here. Would you like to see it?"

"Ah…" he said. "Uh… I suppose."

Tarias stood up and walked toward the room. There was a large bed, far larger than any bed Tarias had ever slept in, with green covers. There was plenty of space for clothes, and candles were lit in all corners of the room but one. In that corner, a mirror stood. Tarias stopped suddenly. He stared at the mirror. He stared at his face.

"Take a seat, soul seeker," said the elfe's voice behind him.

"May I have some time alone?"

He heard a sigh and the sound of her footsteps walking away. The door closed behind him, and he stared at his reflection. He gravitated toward the mirror. At first, he was a whole leg's length away from it; but slowly, he inched closer and closer until his nose almost grazed it. It had been years since he had last seen his reflection. He avoided it. He did not like it. Truthfully, he could not stand it, but now he had to wake to it every morning.

He had brown eyes and exceptionally clear skin. His head was arrow-shaped, and his hair hung from his scalp down to his shoulders. He had no scars. He had never been cut before. He held his hands up in front of him and stared at them. He turned them over several times; he could not stop. It was like he was stuck in a trance. After a moment, he turned back to the mirror—behind him, he saw the *gasping* Princess Elreina.

He dropped down. His chest rose up and down with violence. His head spun, and he felt as though he was about to vomit. He began to sweat profusely.

Why am I reacting like this? Why am I reacting like this? Why? I did nothing wrong? I did my duty. Thoughts repeated in his head.

The door slammed open. It was the elfe, and she ran over to Tarias. She lifted him and held him at his shoulder.

"Breathe in and out, slowly. Deep breaths," said the elfe.

Tarias did as he was told. He always did as he told. He breathed in slowly and breathed out. He closed his eyes, and soon his heartbeat calmed down.

"Do you need anything?" she asked.

Tarias paused for a few moments. He was unsure of whether he wanted to bring it up.

"Could you cover up or turn the mirror away from me, please?"

She smiled at him. "Of course. Stand up for me."

Tarias did, and the elfe led him to his bed. Once he was secured under the sheets and blankets, she turned to the mirror and tossed a gray robe over it so that Tarias could not see it anymore.

"Anything else, Master?" asked the elfe.

Tarias huffed and gritted his teeth. Why was this so *strange?*

"No, thank you. I wish to be alone."

She bowed and exited the room.

CHAPTER 4

Tarias awoke the next day with a spinning headache. It felt like his neck muscles were bracing his head for some impact. He could not remember if he'd had a nightmare or a good night's sleep that night. He pulled himself out of his gray bed and wandered to the wardrobe in the room. He opened the wardrobe doors, and inside was a plethora of gray robes. The elf grabbed one, and he wrapped himself within it.

He did not let his gaze even graze the mirror. He pushed himself in a hurry out of the room and stood in the main room of the home. The elfe servant was cleaning the cupboards that lined the walls.

"I never asked your name," muttered Tarias.

The servant turned around with a smile. "Oh! My name is Ederra. I was told your name was Tarias. It is a really wonderful name. Many Koroarks were named Tarias."

Tarias's eyes drifted down to the tiled floor. He had a smile on his face, but he did not want Ederra to see it. Ederra extended her hand toward Tarias, and in her palms, he saw a letter.

"This is from your superior. He wants you to meet him at the Statue of Ee'nak."

Tarias bowed. He turned to leave, but she grabbed him by his sleeve, tugging him back and stopping him from moving.

"Where are your sandals? You can't leave a house like this and not have something to protect your feet from the dirt outside!"

She handed him a pair of sandals. Tarias sat down and carefully strapped the sandals onto his feet. He was not used to having much on his feet, but he understood why the elfe had given him the shoes.

He stood and marched out of the home. He turned to the road, and in the distance saw the massive golden Statue of Ee'nak. The walk there was nothing extraordinary. He floated down the winding streets of Aigerua. Every day, Tarias felt as though his mind was inactive and that his body just reacted to his surroundings. He built walls against conscious thought, and he felt protected by these walls.

He made it to the base of the statue. Its feet were in a pool of water, and at the pool's rim were fountain spouts surrounded with the heads of azkozals. The statue was made entirely of gold, and it depicted an elf dressed in an older style of chainmail and segmented plate armor. Three massive fire pits with grated covers used to discard waste surrounded the statue. The elf held two swords in his hands while he looked up to the sky with an indomitable hope.

The elf in the black mask leaned his back on the limestone rim of the pool. Tarias drifted over to him and rested his forearms on the pool's edge. He did not let himself look at the reflective water.

"You have done well, Tarias. I hope you are enjoying the home."

Tarias needed a moment to find the proper response.

"I—I am. Thank you, Master."

"You have done well these past few years. Your effectiveness as a soul seeker has proven you to be quite a reliable asset, so I am going to allow you more autonomy. You have earned it."

Tarias bowed his head.

"You have not met any of the other soul seekers yet, so you do not know the difference in skill between them and yourself. From once you started, until now, they would have ended your life in only a second."

Tarias's eyes darted to the elf.

"You are better than them in raw swordplay, but they have a skill that far outweighs yours."

The elf grabbed Tarias's hand, and after Tarias blinked, he noticed that they were now on top of one of the buildings that surrounded the Statue of Ee'nak. There was less black smoke than the last time the elf had done this.

"Channeling."

"Channeling?" Tarias asked.

"Channeling is the ability to manipulate the world around you. The ability to move things to and fro. The ability to see things in the mind that are invisible to the regular eye. The ability to calm, and the ability to wreak havoc."

"Do I have this ability?"

"Not yet. Sit."

The two sank to their knees.

"Close your eyes and remove every thought from your mind. Let there be nothing in your head, not even the thought of pure darkness."

Tarias closed his eyes, but he could not shake away his thoughts. His body did not shake with aggravation, but his mind did boil with it.

"Open your eyes."

Tarias opened his eyes. He looked around. Nothing had changed, and he felt failure stir in his stomach. Elves still roamed the streets, and the Statue of Ee'nak still stood with poise over them. Tarias turned his head back to the black-masked elf.

"What is it you wish for me to see?"

He extended his hand. "Take it, Tarias."

Tarias reached out and put his hand toward the elf's. He stumbled forward a little bit. Tarias shook his head with confusion; he'd never known himself to be clumsy. How could he have missed the elf's hand? He reached for it once more.

His hand went straight through the elf's. Tarias stood up, and the black-masked elf did as well. The elf grabbed Tarias's hand. Tarias stared down at it with wonder. Was he somehow controlling whether or not Tarias could touch him? Did he have the power to make himself intangible?

They were now back in the streets of Aigerua. People were walking all around them, but they walked as if Tarias and the black-masked elf were not there. They did not look at them at all, almost like the two did not exist. The black-masked elf pulled Tarias through the crowds, but an elf bumped Tarias, sending him stumbling back. Tarias shook his head—never before had he been pushed like that in the streets—and regained his footing. He stepped forward, ready to confront the elf, but the elf's eyes were halfway through a blink. He stood with one foot in the air, the other foot firmly planted behind him. His arms were frozen in mid-swing. Tarias walked around the elf and stared at him; with the way he was standing, he should not have been able to balance himself on one foot.

Tarias spun around. Everyone was frozen. He sped through the crowds, and after a moment of looking at every individual to make sure he was not going mad, he turned to find the elf in the black mask. He appeared right in front of him.

"Something is troubling you, Tarias."

"What?"

"We are inside your head. I can tell something is troubling you. It is something new, something that was not there before."

Tarias stared down at his feet as the black-masked elf came closer. His face was immediately to the side of Tarias's.

"Get over it, Tarias." The elf's voice was monotone.

Tarias stared forward.

"I will not have a task for you for some time. In this downtime, you need to get your head together. You are capable of doing everything I have done before you, but not with your mind out of focus."

Tarias opened his eyes. The two of them had returned to the top of the building. The black-masked elf nodded to Tarias and disappeared into a puff of smoke. Tarias stood up and stared at the side of the building while he looked for a route down. He climbed slowly back down to the street.

He knew what was bothering him, but he did not know why. He could not have done anything wrong. It was what he was supposed to do. He clenched his fists so hard his knuckles began to ache, and he sped past the rest of the elves on the road. His mind was a spinning gale of arrows. It hurt to think, so Tarias refused to do so. Instead, he forced his feet to the nearest temple.

The Grand Temple of Aigerua was one of the holiest sites in Aigerua, second only to the Palace itself. It was made of gray stone, and at its edges were trimmed with gold. Its roofs were bulbous and stained with a yellow-gold wash. The priests wore a similar yellow-gold color, and their robes shawled over their left shoulders and hung to cover the entirety of their lower body. All of them had olive-tan skin, and some had lined the road to the entrance of the temple with the cloth hanging off their left shoulder falling to their side. These particular priests were exceptionally well-built, and they each carried a staff in their left hand. They stared at Tarias while he walked past them.

Tarias entered the temple. At the end of the room was a large statue of an elf with the wings of a bat. It was made entirely of gold, and four arms protruded from its sides. The first hand had its palm facing the sky, and on it sat a collection of ripe fruit. The second hand held a hammer. The third held a sword, and a priest stood beside it, gauging its sharpness by cutting it against loose leaves. The fourth hand was empty. It was an open palm facing forward, displayed as if it were asking for an offering. Tarias sped forward and fell to his knees before the statues. He ducked his head down and reached his hands forward, sitting on his heels. He felt the eyes of the elves around him rest on his back. He felt as if they knew what he had done.

"What troubles you, elf of the South?"

Tarias straightened his torso but kept his gaze down. "I have done my duty, yet I feel in my heart that I have wronged the world."

The priest nodded. "Yes, yes. This is a common feeling amongst you southern elves. It is an issue of your dedication to your duty. The only way I may help is by leading your heart to be more dedicated to your purpose, to your service."

Tarias's face was blank, but within his mind was a tempest of anger and discomfort. He *was* fully committed. He only lived for his duty. The only thing important in his life was his duty as a soul seeker, and yet, somehow, he still was not dedicated enough? How could he possibly dedicate any *more* of his life? He would wake up and train. He would wake up and spy. He would wake up and kill. He killed. What more could he do?

"You are right, venerable priest. Thank you."

This was a proper response, but Tarias did not mean it. He wanted to, but his heart did not align with his words. He stood up and left. There was nothing else for him to do there. His day was bland, and he did what he always did. He trained his body by pushing himself off the ground, pulling himself up walls, and carrying heavy pots and stones while he walked. This sort of training granted him some peace, but only for a moment. Stress on the body would always calm the mind, for the body tended to force itself to the forefront.

That day, he pushed himself far more than usual. Afterward, he dragged himself to the bathhouse. He spent an unreasonable amount of time there; even the old elves whose eyes peered at the ladies for far too long left before he did. He lost himself in the steam and heat. For some time, his mind was clear, but soon his frenzied thoughts returned.

There were too many people here, and he felt their eyes on him. He could not shake the feeling of being watched, and his heart raced. He had to leave. His heart screamed at him to leave, so the soul seeker did, immediately. The sky was not dark yet, but the sun rested on the horizon like a ball on the floor.

He returned to his new home, and Ederra welcomed him. He ordered her to stay out of his room. His bed had been made for him, and he gazed at it for a moment. It was unusual for him to have things done for him, but he did not dwell on it for long. He only wanted to sleep. He tucked himself under the covers and closed his eyes. He opened his eyes back up and peered out the window. It was pitch black outside. He grunted and shifted his body with frustration. He did not sleep that night.

CHAPTER 5

Tarias's dry eyes felt like lemon juice had been squeezed into them. He lugged his tired body around his house. He thought he ought to clean to get his mind out of its madness, but Ederra had already made certain that no dust was left on any surface. The pots were clean, and all of his clothes were neatly folded in his wardrobe. A ceramic cup containing water rested on a table next to his bed. He downed it, and his hands fell to the sides of the tabletop. His fingers *squeezed* it. He shook his head and marched out of his room.

"The princess's funeral is today. Everyone outside is dressed in black and green," said Ederra.

Tarias glanced at the door. His heart tapped on his ribs a little quicker. "Is it? I suppose I ought to wear black today, then."

Before Ederra could respond, Tarias returned to his room and entered his wardrobe. He flipped around his garments and found a black jant. He threw his sleeping garments on the floor and dressed himself; then he stormed past Ederra and out of the house. The streets were full of elves in dark colors and looked like a dark river in the middle of a town. He flowed with the people just like any other drop of water.

The funeral was held at the Palace. Tarias kept to a jog: fast enough to hurry, but not so fast as to draw attention. On top of the green walls of the Palace, there was a cloth overhang that covered the Koroark and his bodyguards. The Koroark stared down with sad, sunken eyes. He wept, as a good father would. Tarias thought this strange, for the Koroark held the position at the peak of the soul seeker chain of command. Why would he weep at the death *he* ordered?

Tarias bumped his way through the crowd and craned his neck to see the body of the princess. She wore a green dress and was lying atop a stone tablet. Her hair flowed beautifully to the sides. A priests stood at each corner of the rectangular tablet. One hummed a song, and the others kept their heads down. They would each alternate in who sang, and eventually, all of them had a turn in being heard. They each held a jar in one of their palms. They stuck their opposite hand into the jar and coated it with a grayish-green pomace. Their eyes closed and they rubbed their hands together. Soon after, they began rubbing the corpse with the pomace. Her skin began to harden, and it transformed into light gray stone. An elf with a chisel walked over to the tablet and carved words into the stone.

Here rests the gracious Princess Elreina. Tarias had wonderful vision, but even he was surprised he could make the words out. The four priests knelt, and each took a corner of the tablet onto one of their shoulders. They stood up and turned back to bring the tablet into the Palace of Aigerua. They entered the Palace's gates. The gates were soon shut, and everyone flocked to the walls to place their mourning hands upon it in solidarity with the Koroark.

An elf dressed in a dark brown jant collapsed to his knees in front of the gate. His fists plummeted into the dirt below him. They anchored him there, and his tears leaked in between them. He looked familiar, but Tarias struggled to recall from where. His face was half-covered. Tarias lurked around to the wall, keeping his head down. He placed his palm on the wall and feigned sadness. He kept the elf in the corner of his eye.

Finally, it came to him. It was the elf who had spoken to the Princess before she shut the door on him. Tarias's vision started to blur, and his eyes felt wet.

He shook away his tears. *Crying?* Why did he start crying? He huffed and lifted his foot slightly, but he stopped himself from thrusting it into the ground below. He knew it would not be appropriate for him to display such a tantrum. He turned back to face the brown-dressed elf. The elf stood up and began to walk away, so Tarias began to tail him.

The elf seemed to be in a hurry, because Tarias had trouble keeping up with him. His strides were quick, like he was late to his wedding or something else of similar importance. Tarias was fast, but it was hard to match the speed of such a desperate elf. He found himself at the entrance of an inn, and he watched as the elf barged through it.

It was not appropriate for people to drink during a funeral, for it was not a celebration; however, this had never stopped anyone from doing so. To blend in, Tarias would need money, so the soul seeker's hands gravitated toward the pockets of the rich Sealandesq elves. He only stole from them, since it would be wrong to steal from the Midlandesq elves. It did not take him very long to attain a full purse, for Tarias had been a pickpocket for as long as he had formed memories.

He entered the inn. There were not many people present, and the elf in the brown jant slouched on a stool while his arms rested on top of the bar counter. The proprietor wore all black, and he bowed upon Tarias's entrance.

"Welcome, good elf! If there is anything you need, do not hesitate to ask!"

Tarias grinned. "I do have something to ask. That elf, the one that just walked in—he seems rather... *glum*. Personally, I do not drink, but I pity him. Whatever he orders, you may put it on my tab."

Tarias turned toward the bar counter.

"As a matter of fact, I do not see a drink yet before him." He tossed the proprietor a coin. "Bring him your most expensive rice wine."

The proprietor bowed. Tarias did not hurry to sit next to the elf. He wanted to wait until he was possessed by the wine. The elf did not question the wine being brought to him. He just downed its contents and stared at the bar counter. He had an olive-tan skin tone common to Midlandesq elves, and he spun his finger around the rim of his glass. Tarias kept on supplying alcohol to the elf, and the elf accepted every drop.

Tarias did not know why he felt compelled to follow this elf. This was not orderly for him to do on his own, but he was drawn to him. His curiosity drove him, and this put fear into the soul seeker. The elf's finger became less coordinated as it spun around the rim, and Tarias took this as a sign to question him.

"A sorrowful day, is it?" asked Tarias.

"Aye. Sorrowful indeed. Are you the lad who is piping all this wine to me?" replied the elf.

Tarias nodded. "You look like you could have used a kind gesture."

"Well, thank you."

The elf did not look at Tarias.

"Are you a firm devout?" Tarias asked.

The elf's finger halted its tracing and grabbed the glass. His hands squeezed with sorrow.

"We were close. I miss her." The elf took another sip from his cup.

"It is a shame when friends go. I can only imagine your pain."

The elf scoffed. "Friends? I wish she and I were only friends. Maybe I would have been spared of this sorrow."

He paused and stared blankly at Tarias. Tarias tried to keep his eyes away from the elf's. The elf looked quickly back to his cup. His shoulders rounded forward, his back forming a shell around his cup, and went back to his quiet. Tarias mustered up a smile and left the elf to his solitude.

Tarias pitied the elf, so he allowed him the rest of the day to enjoy the rest of his life. He sat down in an alleyway and sunk his head to stare at the ground. He was to do nothing, absolutely nothing, for the rest of the day. Then he would follow the elf, and he would question him.

But no one can ever truly do *nothing*. Tarias tried to keep an empty head for as long as he could, but his head could only stay clear for so long. Thoughts always robbed him of his peace of mind. She was pregnant. He had killed a pregnant elfe. But it had to happen. The Emperor saw it necessary for the sake of the Terukians. It *had* to happen.

It had to happen. It had to happen. *It had to happen.*

This thought replayed over and over in his head until the elf in brown stumbled out of the inn in a drunken stupor. It was dark at this hour, and the streets were clear. Tarias got to his feet and tailed the elf. The elf walked towards the more affluent district of Aigerua, but his ability to walk was greatly inhibited by his current state. The drunk elf's foot tapped a stone and he stumbled, barreling to the ground. Tarias rushed toward him with an extended hand.

"Ahh… How fool—iissh of me. I should have seen… that stone!" He grunted.

Tarias nodded. "Worry not, good gentle elf. Let me aid you in returning home."

"Er… No, I… No, thanks. I shall just get going on." The elf stared at Tarias's face. "Have I… seen you before?"

"No, good elf. I don't think so."

"Oh."

"Where do you live, good elf? You are in no state to travel alone."

The elf hiccupped. "I live near the, er… the statue."

Tarias set off towards the Statue of Ee'nak. He dragged the drunk elf along while he looked for a place to question him. He did not know what to expect to find in the elf's house, so he kept his eyes peeled for a hole to hide him in. He saw no one around him.

"I know a shortcut, good elf. Come with me."

Tarias pulled the elf with him. Naturally, the elf provided some resistance; but since the elf was so overtaken by alcohol, this resistance amounted to an easily overpowered outcome. They entered an alleyway. Several boxes were stacked around, and they provided good cover from sight. Tarias pushed the elf behind the boxes, holding him by the neck.

"What is your relation to the princess?" asked Tarias.

The elf stared at Tarias with wide, sad eyes. "What?"

"Your relation to the princess," said Tarias as he tightened his grip around the elf's neck.

Tears began to pour from the elf's eyes. Tarias felt him go limp. Tarias let go of his neck, and the elf wept while he stared at the ground. Tarias knelt and grabbed him by the shoulders.

"What is your relation to her? To Elreina?"

"I loved her. I loved her so much… I regret what I told her before she was taken from the world, and now my heart aches more than I ever knew it could. I thought I lost her yesterday, but now I have lost her for good… I am empty."

Tarias struggled to ask his next question.

"Are you... Are you under the employment of an Ark? Are you going to kill me?"

Tarias stumbled backward and stared at him with a look of shock. "I... I am not going to kill you."

The elf gripped Tarias by the forearms. "Please... *Please* kill me. I have lost everything I cared for. All I have is my trade. I have lost my love, and I have lost my *child*."

Tarias's head said to *run*. He stood up and sped off, ignoring the sounds of weeping behind him. It was not the elf he feared, but rather his own feelings about his plight. He hated his feelings. They made him feel wrong. His heart told him he should have done or said something, but his mind ordered him not to. So he ran. He ran all the way home, slammed open his door, entered his room, and went to sleep.

Shockingly, he had decent sleep that night. He only woke up three times, which was about twice as good as usual. He stood up from his bed and left his room.

"Hello, Tarias," said Ederra.

"Hello."

Tarias felt awkward saying a simple greeting, and he figured he would make some small talk.

"How is the day?"

"It is tragic," Ederra said. "A merchant was found dead in the fountain underneath the Golden Statue's feet. The veins in his arms were slit open, and he lay there to die. Another horrible tragedy."

Tarias stumbled and caught himself by extending his arm to a side table.

"Are you alright, soul seeker?"

"I am… fine."

Tarias left the house and hurried toward the Golden Statue. Elves dressed in armor and green jants stood at one part of it. The water had a red tinge, and a dead elf rested on the ground. He wore a brown jant.

CHAPTER 6

Tarias rushed back to his house. His heart was racing, and he felt a palm slam into his chest. The black-masked elf stood in front of him with his arm extended. Tarias could never tell how the elf felt, if he was angry or proud, and this did not relax his heart at all.

"Walk with me," said the elf.

Tarias would not disobey his superior, so he went forward with the elf.

"What compelled you to speak with that elf?"

"What elf?"

"The one who died this morning."

Tarias stared at the sky. "I saw him weeping. He seemed quite sad about Princess Elreina's death."

"I could tell. He is with her now. Next time, leave things like this alone. You have no reason to go and ask your own questions. You did nothing wrong," said the black-masked elf, resting his hand on Tarias's shoulder.

Tarias blinked, and the elf was gone.

The elf's words did little to help soothe Tarias's woes. There was a disconnect between his ears and heart. In truth, his heart had begun to beat faster than before. He was meant to be calm. It was his job to be ready to act, but his heart shoved him into an anxious state. He wished to calm his mind, so he once more sought out the bathhouse.

He descended into the steamy bathhouse waters. He usually kept his eyes open, but that day, something told him to close them. He finally felt some peace in the water. He heard doors open and close. He felt the ripples of other elves entering, leaving, and moving in the bath. He shivered with discomfort. He felt *watched.*

A young elf, a little bit younger than Tarias, sat next to him in the water. He looked up at the ceiling with a pleasant smile. It was a bit strange to Tarias, but he shook it off. His elbow was bumped. The young elf stared at him.

"Are you… alright?" asked Tarias.

"Oh, I am wonderful!"

Tarias looked around. "You are moving quite a bit. I do not wish to sound rude, but could you please give me some space?"

"Eh. You have plenty of space, it seems."

The elf continued to stare at Tarias. He had olive-tan skin and hazel eyes. His hair hung down to his shoulders, but it was tied in the back. His smile was cocky and annoying. He certainly had the mind of a child.

"Lad, I am having a rough time right now, and I wish for a bit of peace. Could you *please* give me some space?"

The elf smirked. "Space? You don't think you deserve it. Do you?"

Tarias grimaced. He stood up and looked down at the boy. Suddenly, his head started to ache. He clutched it. It felt like it was being hammered in by a mallet. He gritted his teeth and scrunched his fingers until they stung with tension.

"Gah! I'm sorry, I—I must go. My head is aching."

Tarias opened his eyes and saw that he was suddenly in a limbo. Black smoke emanated from the ground below him, and a long stretch of empty void was all that could be seen up in the sky and at the horizon. His eyes were open wide.

The boy stood before him. Tarias got a better look at his features. He was thin, without the brawn of a fully grown elf, and stood a hair taller than Tarias. He had olive-tan skin, wore a crimson jant, and his feet were bare while they rested on the smoky black clouds below. His grin was as sly as any know-it-all brat, and he stood motionless with the same unsettling glare.

"What's the matter. Tarias? Have you suddenly lost your nerve?"

"What? You know my name. How—"

Tarias paused. He knew full well what was happening at that moment. *The elf was in his head.*

"Yes, Tarias. I am," said the elf.

"What is your name?"

His sly grin grew closer to his ears. "Apparently, you think you are a soul seeker. Should you not know how foolish it is to ask my name?"

Before Tarias could respond, it felt like his head was filled with the pressure of a volcano that had been dormant for far too long. He tried to claw into his own head to take the pain away, but it refused to vacate. He stared up at the elf as he fell to his knees.

"Strange."

The pain ceased. Tarias looked around in a frenzy.

"What? What do you mean, strange?"

The elf's smirk was gone. He sat down with his legs crossed. He stared at the ground, his brow furrowed, deep in thought.

"You feel guilt," he said.

Tarias shook his head. "Guilt? What do you mean?"

The elf raised his head. "Who ordered you to kill the Princess?"

Tarias kept his mouth shut.

"I see. We are going to have to do this the *traditional* way."

The black smoke faded away as the world came back to Tarias. His face was slammed into the rim of the bathhouse pool. Tarias saw stars, stunned by the pain. He felt his arms being grabbed, so he spun in an attempt to undo the tightness in his shoulder. He sent a jab at the elf and followed it up with the tip of his right elbow. It looked as if he was cutting sideways with a sword, and he connected square into the face of the elf.

The elf recovered and tried to counter, but Tarias had already climbed out of the bath. He pulled on a random robe that hung on the wall and sprinted out of the doors. The elf did the same, and the two pierced through the crowds of people that traveled the streets. Tarias did not care to stick to the sides of the road this time, even though his skin was bare for all to see, and he kept going despite the foul looks that followed him like a poor body odor. The elf was right behind him. He was far faster than the average elf, and he rivaled Tarias's own speed. Tarias kept his head forward, for he did not want to have the worried thoughts of being caught slow him down. He climbed on top of a building, hopped over rooftops, and slid down back to another road. The elf followed him. Tarias could not shake him. Whatever Tarias did, the elf would do just as well. He was just like him. He was undoubtedly a soul seeker as well.

Tarias felt a rock slam into his shoulder, and he was sent forward toward the floor. He tucked his shoulder and rolled while he maintained momentum, but he hit a ledge that stopped him from going forward. The elf ran up to him and shot forward to pin him down, but Tarias rolled sideways. Again, the elf turned to Tarias to pin him, but Tarias wrestled up and got his arms around the elf's leg. He put the elf's foot on the crook of his elbow and pulled on his knee; then he turned and kicked the elf's leg out from under him. He held him down, slamming his fists into the elf's face. He stuck his arm under his head and shoved his shoulder onto one side of his neck. The elf's shoulder pressed on his own neck on the other side, kept in place by Tarias's head. Tarias *squeezed*. He kept on squeezing. It was slow yet unrelenting. The elf fought less and less; but suddenly, Tarias's arms closed on empty air.

Did he escape? How had he slipped out? Tarias's frenzied head looked down and saw that he was choking on black smoke. He got to his feet and watched the smoke wisp away into the wind. He ran.

He ran back to his house. The elf certainly was not in a condition to pursue him if he had displaced himself as Tarias thought. He was probably near passing out, or maybe he *had* passed out. Even further, his head was too badly beaten to run straight; nonetheless, Tarias still kept his head on a swivel, for maybe the elf was also adept at self-healing. He was certainly gifted with a few tricks.

He entered his door to see Ederra resting on a chair. Her legs were crossed, and she read a scroll in her hands. She turned her head to Tarias with a wide smile.

"Welcome home, Tarias."

Tarias gave her a quick smile and hurried to his room. He knew she listened to the elf with the black mask first—she *had* to—so he decided to keep his experiences that day to himself. He knew should have told her, but a voice in the back of his head told him not to.

He stared at the mirror in the corner of the room. He knew his reflection was behind the draped gray cloak that covered it. A burning feeling filled him from the depths of his gut. The bottom of his throat felt strangely full, like he had trouble swallowing mucus. He felt these feelings when he looked in the mirror. It was the mirror. It was certainly the mirror causing these feelings. He grabbed its sides and spun it around so that the reflective side faced the corner.

Seeing that the cloak did not need to cover up the mirror any longer, he lifted it off.

Tarias sat down on the side of his bed, and Ederra entered his room.

"You are a peculiar elf, Tarias."

Tarias turned his head to Ederra with a questioning stare until he noticed Ederra looking him up and down. He smirked once he caught on.

"I misplaced my clothes in the bathhouse and had to pilfer new garments. Is that strange to you?" he asked.

"Maybe not for the average person, but I thought soul seekers were more… well… *diligent.*"

Tarias grimaced. She was right.

"I was found."

Ederra's eyes went wide. "What do you mean, *found?*"

"Another soul seeker attempted to enter my thoughts and obtain information from me. Information about our superior."

"*Your* superior. You are my superior."

"That cannot be. That is absurd. I am no superior."

Ederra inched closer. "Did you tell the soul seeker anything?"

"No. But…" He stopped himself from speaking further.

"But what?"

"He knew my name."

"You said he *attempted* to enter your thoughts, yet he knows your name? What else does he know?"

Ederra's movements grew more erratic. She looked out of the door of Tarias's room as if she were listening for something. Tarias stood up and placed a hand on her shoulder. She turned and moved her palm to shove it off, but she stopped it in midair.

"Did you kill him?" she asked.

"No."

"Then how are you sure he did not follow you?"

"I beat him in a fight, and he had to flee by displacing himself. He was in no condition to pursue me any longer."

Ederra turned her head and left the room. She stared out the window. She was close enough to see outside, but also far enough away to not be noticed by any passersby. She had goosebumps on her shoulders. Tarias gazed at her for far longer than was acceptable. His gaze descended. He closed his eyes and brought himself back to reality.

"We must report this to our—*my* superior. That soul seeker needs to be killed," Tarias said.

"For both of our sakes, you must. Let us hope he reveals himself to you again soon."

"The only thing we can do now is wait."

Tarias walked back to his room and shut the door behind him. He extinguished every candle and lay flat on his bed. He tried to shut his eyes, but they taunted him with their rebellion. He felt tired, but his body refused to listen. Why had the elf been unable to delve deeper into his head? Tarias knew he was not skilled in that area, so of course he should not have been able to resist as well as he had. Had he resisted? He dwelled on these thoughts, circling in his mind like a tearing whirlpool.

CHAPTER 7

"Rise."

It sounded like a command from the heavens. Tarias opened his eyes, and a black mask hovered over his face. Tarias clawed himself out of bed and onto the floor. He knelt in front of the elf.

"I suppose Ederra has told you of what happened," said Tarias.

"What happened?" asked the elf.

Ederra stood in the corner of the room. Tarias whipped his head to her, then he looked back to the elf in the black mask.

"She told you nothing?"

"No. Spit it out."

Tarias briefed his superior about what had happened the day prior. The elf stood back and leaned on the dresser, propping himself up with his palms. He looked up toward the ceiling. His mask made it hard to tell what he was feeling, but Tarias could see he was not worried. He never looked worried. He would often pause, as he was doing now, and deliberate on how to proceed. He was a thinker.

"Tarias. You are to stay secluded in this building. You will command Ederra to tend to all of your needs. I can sense that your mind is still disordered. Handle that. You are useless to me until you do, and you certainly will not be able to combat this soul seeker further."

Tarias bowed, and the elf in the black mask displaced himself away. For the next seven days and seven nights, he did exactly what he was ordered to do. He secluded himself within the walls of his home. Ederra would bring him food and water, and Tarias accepted his meals with grace. He attempted to keep himself fit within his dwelling by moving his body in unorthodox ways, as well as by using household objects as weights. This helped him keep the thoughts of guilt away. Ederra would start a bath for him every night, and at first, he was reluctant to let her wash him; but as the days went on, he grew more open to it. He enjoyed it.

After the seventh day passed, his seclusion began to feel more like a prison than a time to relax. That night, when Ederra started his bath, he looked down to the water and saw his face, and soon the feelings of guilt-filled dread corroded his mind. The face of Princess Elreina stabbed his thoughts. The bath water looked to be filled with blood, and the image of the princess's dead lover overwhelmed him. He jumped out of the bath and ran to the wall with a table along it. He bore his weight on his hands, leaning over the table while he gasped for air. He felt *defective*. He felt heavier than he should have. He could not shake the fact that something was wrong with him. He should *not* have been feeling this way. He was in perfect health. He was a well-maintained weapon. It was his duty to keep his body healthy.

Ederra ran in and gasped. She covered him with a towel and rubbed his back. He shooed her away and tucked the corner of the towel at his waist. He paced around the room and regained his composure. This episode had been less severe than the last, and he thought maybe he was getting a bit better. Maybe he was dealing with some strange affliction, and now, finally, he was recovering from it.

The next week was far more somber. Most of it was the same, but at night the thoughts continued to bombard him. He was losing sleep. He longed to be outside, but he kept himself within his dwelling. He had been ordered to stay, so he stayed. He felt a pull from the outside, but he could not let himself leave. He would not leave.

The week after that was *far* worse than the two previous. He did not get any sleep. His stomach churned and its contents erupted out of his throat several times. His head spun, and it felt like a hammer was constantly banging on his crown. He stumbled over his own feet often, and he could barely see through the haze that covered his eyes. Not only that, the temptation to leave grew even more enticing. He figured he was ill, but with what? Ederra tended to him with every herb or remedy imaginable, but he only grew worse.

Once the week had passed, he could not convince himself to stay any longer. The urge had grown too strong, so he put on one of his gray robes and fled his prison. Ederra tried to remind him of his superior's command, but once she saw the look in his eyes, she held her tongue.

Tarias took a walk. The smell of fresh air stabilized his head for a moment. The colors of the city felt new to him again, and this revived novelty allowed him to focus on something other than what plagued his mind. He walked to his favorite part of town. Plenty of food stalls lined these streets, and curtains hung down advertising the names of the establishments that served the public.

Tarias entered his favorite eatery. The owner greeted him with a bow and led him to his seat.

"Thank you for your consistent hospitality. I will bring over a few of your kurros rolls and some ona noodles."

The owner bowed, and he ran off to the counter and yelled for the order to be made. Tarias leaned back in his chair and smiled. It felt good to finally be out of the house again. After moments of patient waiting, his food was brought out to him. The crunchy texture of the rolls pleased his mouth, and once he finished those, he could not stop himself from enjoying the brothy noodles. He finished them and bowed his head to the table. The owner came up to him.

"How was your meal, gentle elf?"

"It was extraordinary! You never do disappoint me here!"

The owner smiled. "I am glad you enjoyed it. Your dessert will be coming up shortly."

Tarias shook his head. "What dessert?"

"An elf up there at the counter ordered some of your favorite butter cookies for you. He said he was your friend. A good friend he is!"

Tarias looked up to the counter, and he saw the smile of the cocky young soul seeker. Every urge within him told him to run, but where would he go? The elf knew this place was Tarias's favorite, and he even knew his favorite dessert. He needed to find out what else he knew. The elf waltzed over to Tarias's table.

"It is not often that I see you, Tarias! It is such a pleasure seeing you again."

That damned cocky smile taunted Tarias.

"Yes… It is always a pleasant experience to be had with you," Tarias said.

"I do not wish to get in the middle of your reunion," said the owner of the restaurant. "I will be off."

He retreated behind the bar counter, and the other soul seeker sat down on the chair opposite Tarias. He extended his hand to him. It was as if he wanted Tarias to shake his hand. Tarias looked at it with concern.

"Worry not. There is no catch with touching my hand."

Hesitating, Tarias shook the elf's hand.

"Songas."

"Songas?"

"That is my name."

Tarias leaned forward. "Why are you telling me your name? Do you not see how stupid it is to tell me your name if you want to kill me?"

Songas laughed. "I do not want to kill you."

Tarias fell back to the rail of his chair and shot his arms up. "Then what do you want from me?"

The owner walked out with a large plate of butter cookies in his hand. He placed them in front of the two soul seekers and left with a smile. Songas grabbed one of the cookies and placed it in his mouth. He smiled at the taste of them and beckoned Tarias to have some.

"I want you to enjoy some of these cookies."

Tarias stared at them. He grabbed one of them and ate it.

"What else?"

The elf smiled with creases in his eyes. "Why must there be something else?"

"There is always something else."

Songas's grin dissipated, and the two ate the rest of the cookies in silence. Songas stood up and beckoned Tarias to follow, but Tarias stayed put in his seat. The elf looked annoyed and sat back down in the chair across from Tarias.

"I am not going anywhere with you," said Tarias.

The two stared at each other for an uncomfortable period of time. Tarias simmered with hot frustration. He wished to leave, yet he feared Songas following him and attempting to pluck him from the streets and into some hidden hole to be interrogated and tortured. His curiosity made his leg bounce. What if Songas truly did not wish to kill Tarias? But he knew it was foolish to believe the soul seeker—they were known for lies—so he sat down and waited.

Songas leaned forward. "You know just as well as I do that your mind is too chaotic for me to pluck anything from your thoughts. I have no reason to harm you, Tarias."

"But you do have reason to interrogate and torture me, no?"

"No. I do not. As you have seen, I have been able to pluck thoughts from your head, but they were very random. There was no form or sense to them. One of the first thoughts... Are you familiar with the phrase *I am a tool?*"

Tarias's heart beat with an anxious rhythm. His vision became a tunnel with Songas at the epicenter. He wanted to hurt him, but he did not know why. It was the truth; Tarias was a tool. He was nothing other than a simple tool for his superior. He used that phrase for comfort, but why did it pain him to hear it from another person's lips?

"Fine." Tarias stood up and walked out from under the restaurant's curtains.

Songas followed him, and to Tarias's amazement, he did not immediately pull a blade. They walked the streets of Aigerua without speaking to one another. They traveled a few blocks, and all the while, Tarias shook with the fear that the elf with the black mask might notice his actions. He flooded other thoughts into his head out of fear that Songas would catch on to his worries.

"Where are you from?" Songas asked.

Tarias shook his head. "You know just as well as I that you are trying to build rapport with me right now. What is your intention, Songas?"

"To get to know you," Songas said. "I will not lie. I truly do wish to find your superior, but I have my own will, freedom, and personal missions."

Will? Freedom? Personal missions? Tarias could not believe this was a soul seeker.

"You believe a soul seeker is only a tool. I was not lying when I said you were not a soul seeker. You are not."

Tarias wanted to yell and hit Songas for saying such stupid words. "What makes you think you are any more a soul seeker than I? I have dedicated my entirety to my superior. Everything I have ever done was in service of my duty."

"You do not know what a soul seeker is. A soul seeker is not devoted to their *superior*. A soul seeker is devoted to the Terukian people. They will do what is *right* for them."

"How do your personal passions help you with that? Where is your guidance?"

Songas sighed. The two continued walking down the streets until the Palace of Aigerua came into view. Songas stood and stared at the palace.

"How does killing the princess aid the Terukian people?"

Tarias did not answer.

"You never asked yourself that question, did you? Or maybe you did not wish to ponder over it for too long for the sake of your own *declining* sanity."

He had asked himself that same question. He *hated* that he had asked himself that question.

"It was what the Koroark willed," Tarias said.

Songas laughed. "Did you hear the Koroark speak that from his own tongue, or did you hear that from your superior? Who are you to think you know the will of the Koroark?"

Tarias shook his head. "My superior takes his orders from the Koroark."

Songas scoffed. "That may be so, but I *also* take my orders from the Kororark."

Tarias laughed. He shook his head. He shook his head until this thought disappeared. Songas was certainly lying to him; he must have been one of the rebel soul seekers the elf in the black mask had told him about. The elf in the black mask had stood *next* to the Koroark the night of the assassination. He was one of his closest soldiers. Songas angered him with his insinuations. Tarias stormed off, away from Songas.

"Where are you going?"

"Away from your foul words."

CHAPTER 8

It had been four days since Tarias disobeyed the order to stay in his home. He heard nothing from the black mask within those four days, and Ederra said nothing of it to him. After coming home, he returned to the same routine he had succumbed to prior, until he awoke on the fifth day to the feeling of being shaken in his bed.

He looked up and saw Ederra. She was beautiful as always, with her black hair swept to the side. He had grown more accustomed to appreciating her beauty, and the perceived taboo seemed to wear away. He felt her continue to shake him. Her lips moved, but, distracted by her pretty face, it took him a moment to understand what she was saying.

"He is here! Wake up!"

Tarias shook himself awake. He rose and shot out of his room. The elf with the black mask was present, and he sat down on one of Tarias's chairs waiting for him. As always, Tarias had trouble figuring out his mood. He stood up, and Tarias awaited what he had to say. The elf took his time. He did not move like he was stressed or in a rush.

"I have a new target for you, Tarias. It has been long enough, and you will not be bothered by that rebel soul seeker any longer. The elf you are going to kill is a gong farmer in the Yellow Aucs."

Tarias shuttered at the thought of having to deal with the smell of shit, but he was a soul seeker. He was supposed to get his hands dirty.

"You will kill him while he is doing his job in the old Yellow Aucs sewers. It will be the best place to get rid of him, for there will be no one else around to witness it. You can be as loud as you wish. I do not care."

"What is his post and description?"

"He is tasked with clearing the muck at the southernmost sewer hole in the Aucs. He is a middle-aged elf and will be the only one present. You will kill him tonight. Be swift, Tarias."

Tarias bowed, and the black masked elf displaced himself away.

"Ederra, would you be so kind as to run a bath for me? No need for any pleasant-smelling soaps—leave them for when I come home."

"Of course, Master," replied Ederra.

She ran him a bath, and Tarias made sure to enjoy it. He thanked the Koroark that he was finally going on another mission. Novelty had a way of taking his mind off of his suffering. He took his time with his bath. The child within him urged him to use his fingers to trace little waves in the tub of the water. It helped his mind in two ways: it cured his immature boredom, and the ripples disfigured his reflection. A good chunk of the day had fizzled away from him while he let his thoughts drift away in the waves of the bath water.

He rose from the tub and reached for the nearest towel to wipe the water from himself. The water dripped from his chest, and he caught a glimpse of his figure in the reflection of the now calm bath water. He closed his eyes immediately and ventured to cover himself. He exited his bathroom.

"Thank you Ederra," said Tarias while his hand reached the handle of his door.

"You are welcome, Master Tarias. I will always have your bath ready when needed," she replied with a smile.

Tarias returned her smile and left. It still felt foreign to be called Master, but dwelling on it only spun his mind into a frenzy. He could not afford to have that happen on a task, so he decided to shove those thoughts into one of the many deep chasms in his mind. The Yellow Aucs was a long walk from where he stayed, so he went right on to his task. As with every task, he kept his head down and his eyes alert. Songas was on his mind, but he did not worry about it. The thought that their talk might have been a plot to bring his guard down struck him, but he shrugged it off.

The streets were bustling with activity like any other day, but the center of the road was less dense with people. The Yellow Aucs did not see many Midlandesq elves, for it was too far away from the palace and too smelly for them to bear. The hammering of steel echoed from the large warehouses and crafts shops. The roads in the Yellow were far grayer and more gravelly than the finely paved roads in the center of Aigerua. He walked down these roads until he spotted the sewer hole.

His eyes wandered, looking for a place to wait. He knew gong farmers hated how their profession forced them to smell, so the task would only be possible in the evening. Tarias spotted a noodle shop.

It was in the perfect location. It was right across the street from the sewer hole, and it had an exterior bar that allowed customers to face the road. He marched straight for it. The owner there sat him down, and he soon received some appetizers. An indecisive elf would spend a long time trying to figure out what to eat from the menu, and Tarias was so *generously* indecisive that night. But it would be strange for him to stay at a restaurant all day. The occasional picky customer was understandable; but the customer that did not leave would not be an everyday problem. Tarias figured after his second entrée that he had sat there for too long, so he left and went back to the streets.

He lay down on the ground. It was not uncommon to see the occasional elf sleeping on the streets in the Yellow, so no one batted an eye at Tarias. His head rested in a manner that coincidentally faced the sewer hole. He waited. It was reaching evening, so his target would soon be heading over to his own task. He felt pity for the elf, not because he cleaned the shit out of sewers, but because he would die in one tonight.

"I am a tool," Tarias muttered as he attempted to scare off his pity.

Moments later, an elf dragged his feet to the sewer hole. He stared at it for several moments until finally obtaining the courage to lift the sewer cover. Once it was up, he hurried himself and his tools down. Tarias noticed he had carried with him an assortment of tools, ranging from a large shovel to smaller scrapers. Tarias's weapon would be whichever of those that first fell into his hands. He stayed on the floor; eager elves were always the ones to mess up with tasks like these. The consequences of one slip-up would be far more severe than a slap on the wrist.

After the sky started to redden with the sun on the horizon, Tarias went for the sewer hole and climbed down. It stank like *shit*. There was not a more colorful word to describe the stench. It simply stank of shit. The muffled sounds of steel hitting bricks sounded off in an irregular pattern down the sewer. He heard the excrement *plop* on the ground and a frustrated moan. Tarias turned the corner and spotted the gong farmer placing down his scraper in favor of his shovel to get rid of his mistake. Tarias rushed forward, his legs moving swiftly in the direction of the elf. He reached for the scraper, but the wooden shaft of the shovel struck him in the head.

"You fucking wretch," said the gong farmer.

Tarias looked up, and he then felt his knee cave in from behind. He fell to his knees. He wrapped his arms around both of the shit scraper's thighs and used his head to off-balance him while he threw him to the ground. Tarias spun around, and several elves all armed with bludgeons and knives surrounded him. He stumbled back with shock. He moved his head left, then right, left again, then he ducked, grabbing the arm of the closest elf and slamming his wrist into the wall. He expected the elf to wince in pain from how hard he had slammed the elf's hand into the brick wall, but there was a thick layer of crap covering it. The elf cringed in disgust, Tarias used this moment to strip his bludgeon from him and whack him over the head. He fell into the flow of excrement in the center of the sewer tunnel. A knife struck forward towards Tarias's face, sending him in another stumble backward. The torches his aggressors held only made the smell worse, and Tarias caught an even worse whiff of his surroundings as they came closer. It stunned him for a moment, and he felt a sharp, bruising pain in his right rib.

"Fuck!"

He choked the bludgeon in his hands and swung. He hit the elf in front of him dead on the chin. Because of the geography of the tunnel, only one person could attack Tarias at a time, but this changed once Tarias heard the footsteps running behind him. He pushed the elves in front of him backwards, sending them tumbling and falling over one another, and reached for the shovel that rested below him. He held the shovel in his hands like a spear and jutted it forward at the elves. He struck one in the neck. The footsteps grew louder, so Tarias turned his head and sent the butt of the shovel behind him into the forehead of an elf. Back and forth he spun and stabbed with his shovel, and repeatedly his enemies fell, but they kept on coming.

Why were there so many of them? Tarias asked himself.

The soul seeker started to feel his arms grow tired from the stabbing and his legs sore from the constant spinning. He could only maintain his quick reflexes for so long until he would be forced to move more slowly. He looked around in search of an escape. A knife zipped past him, and he looked down to see his arm cut and bleeding. His mind was too chaotic to fight *and* think of a way out, but he could not let the thought of failure consume him. Hopefully, his enemies would run out before his body failed him. Elves fell front-and-back, back-and-front, while Tarias's energy drained from him. *How were there so many of them?*

The soul seeker collected more and more wounds as the fight went on, which slowed him down even more. His enemies were dying, but by now, there seemed to be more elves in the sewers than *shit*. Tarias had gotten used to the stench at this point, but he lost track of time. He *had* to keep on fighting.

Then his thoughts wandered. Who were these people? How did they know he was there? Who was the elf he was supposed to kill? Why was this happening? *How* had this happened? *Who had betrayed him?* Like all the other thoughts in his head, these thoughts struck him in quick succession. His focus started to wander, distracting him from tracking the scene before him. He slowed down his movements even further, trying to regain his composure, but his thoughts were whipping around in angry winds. His mind was, at that moment, *obsessed* with his thoughts—until a club struck him in the head, knocking him unconscious.

CHAPTER 9

Tarias woke up to the starry night sky. He turned his head side-to-side, gazing at the landscape around him. He was surrounded by blades of grass, yet he still smelled the shit of the sewers he had been fighting in. Once he lifted his head to look forward, he saw an elf sitting down on the hill watching the city in front of him. The elf turned his head.

"Songas? What? Was it you?" asked Tarias.

Songas frowned. "No. It was not."

Tarias sat up, but when he attempted to support his torso with his arm, he collapsed back to the ground. He muttered *'fuck'* and lay there for a moment. He suddenly felt as though he had nothing. He had never felt like he had anything before, but now, he truly felt that he had no possessions, nor home, nor sense of belonging to anything. It gave him some peace of mind. His eyes drifted back to Songas. *Why did he help me? How did he know?*

"It was the Koroark who ordered your death. He was given evidence of your next target by another of the Eskus."

"What? What's an Esku?"

Songas gave the same sly smirk he always had on his face. "Another reason why you aren't truly a soul seeker. I am an Esku—and your 'superior' is one, too."

Tarias's eyes widened. His superior? Could he have been set up by the elf in the black mask? He dragged himself painfully into a position where he sat on his heels. It had to have been the elf in the black mask, as he was the only one with access to the Emperor; but *why?* Even further, why would Songas help?

"You… You went against the Emperor's order?"

Songas laughed. "Oh, heavens no! That would be stupid. I was never ordered to kill you; I was ordered to find out who your superior was. I cannot do that if you are dead in a sewer.

The Emperor ordered whoever gave him the information to execute you. I believe that the Esku who gave him the evidence of your whereabouts is your superior."

Tarias felt like he was staring down into a tunnel. His whole world felt like it was crumbling around him. So, it *was* him. Tarias sat down with a long stare, set dead on Aigerua. He had been betrayed, and his heart had beaten faster while he struggled to cope with the idea of it. He looked at Songas. Maybe his superior had seen him with Songas and wished to execute him for his disobedience. He could not fault his superior, Tarias reasoned, for he had acted out of line. Songas ducked his head and snickered as if he heard Tarias's thought.

"Are you still poking around my head?" Tarias asked.

"You are such a brainwashed fool. Get your head out of the shit you stuck it in."

Tarias snarled at Songas, yet he did not speak against him. His face sank with the realization that he truly had been deceived. He still felt that he could not fault his superior, for Tarias's purpose was deceit and murder. He had no other merits, whether it be in learned skills or natural talents, so how would it not be hypocritical to be angry with his superior for lying to him?

Songas shot up and threw a rock down the steep hill. "Damn it, Tarias! Stop thinking this foolishness! Stop telling yourself how *right*, or *okay*, or *permissible* it was for your superior to plan your *death*. He has been using you for the most nefarious of acts, but you afford no thought to him ordering you to kill the daughter of the Koroark!"

"I am not supposed to ask *why*. It is not the tool's place to ask," he muttered.

"Why not? You are going to kill them, yet you do not find it worthwhile to know the reason why they are to die? Is that not useful information? Is it not useful to know every fact to devise the best plan to kill? Height, appearance, skin tone, hair color, if she is with child—"

"I did not know!" shouted Tarias.

Songas closed his mouth. He turned around and sat down once more to stare at Aigerua. He wrapped his arms around his crisscrossed legs. It was so quiet that it was *loud*. After a moment, Songas nodded his head and smiled.

"You are not a bad person, Tarias. You are a hurt person."

Tarias grimaced for a moment, but it quickly dissipated into a stare that went through the ground. He felt flames being lit within his gut. He had been taught that these types of thoughts were poison to the mind. They were meant to be discarded into the cesspit of the head and never to be thoroughly considered. It was a vice to think about the *rightness* or *wrongness* of his actions, for it blinded one from following orders.

Tarias attempted to claw himself up from the dirt he had been relegated to. His fatigued and slashed muscles quivered with a panic that made it seem as though his muscles feared to move from his spot on the hill. This elf was filling his already overflowing skull with too many off-limits ideas. He crumbled under their weight and cursed to himself. He had forgotten the last time he felt so weak, and this event dug into the depths of his head.

He remembered the kicking: repetitive, relentless, malicious, *pointless* kicking. Like flurries of snow, he was pelted all over with beatings. There was nothing he could do. *Powerless* was the only word he could use to describe himself. The feeling of his head being slammed into the gravel streets that day struck him with the same vigor. His memories gave him physical pain. He looked up and saw a hand reaching out for him. The elf who owned the hand wore a black mask.

Tarias's vision faded. The elf's mask vanished and revealed the somber face of Songas. The elf's attire immediately altered as well, but the hand was still extended, beckoning him to accept his aid. Tarias accepted his open palm. The other soul seeker slung his arm over Tarias's shoulder and started his walk back to Aigerua. He dragged Tarias through the Terukian countryside.

"How can you read my thoughts?" Tarias asked.

Songas frowned. "I don't read them. I experience them."

Tarias's brows raised. At first, he was repulsed, then he was ashamed, and finally, he felt pity for Songas.

"I apologize for my thoughts. I cannot control them."

Songas laughed. "You are kind. I could kill you to make them stop, but… you are too *kind*."

'Kind' was not a word that Tarias would have used to describe himself. Whatever kindness he had died long ago. The world was not kind. He had to kill those who harmed the world—that was what his superior had taught him. Guilt flooded into his heart, and Tarias felt it pump throughout his body. He felt the guilt all over. He felt the same bruises he was dealt when he was younger, and it stemmed from the thought of becoming what he hated most.

He had become what harmed the world. Led astray by the young need for belonging and acceptance, his hand had morphed into the knife that stabbed those just like him. He felt heavier, and Songas labored with more effort to continue to carry him forward.

"You used to be useful to someone. Be useful to yourself, instead, and stop being dead weight; or maybe if you still feel the need to serve someone, just help me carry you back."

Tarias had not realized how fatigued Songas was. His skin was paler than he remembered, and he had a strange sweaty musk to him. He licked his lips often—his mouth must have been dry—and his eyes were sunken. Tarias clenched his jaw at the thought of being useless, so he used his strong leg to help hop himself along.

The gates of Aigerua, with their brown stone bricks, stood with a boastful posture. They were closed, and the night sky did not have enough shine to give its golden gates any luster. They trudged their way through the grass to avoid the roads. A smart choice, obviously, as Tarias would have been apprehended on the spot. Undoubtedly, he was a wanted elf at this point. Songas nodded to Tarias's thoughts. They walked to the wall, Tarias blinked, and then they were inside the walls of the capital.

Displacement was a strange feeling. It felt like every fiber of Tarias's being was being disassembled and reassembled; fast, but not immediate. It was quicker than a blink, but he still felt his skin, bones, organs, and thoughts drift apart from each other. It was uncomfortable, not painful. The matter that composed him rubbed against itself—like the feeling when one's nails rubbed against a rough surface, like rock or cork. He felt every bit of himself dissolve into the wind and *through* objects, just to come back together and deliver him the same rubbing feeling. Tarias was set down to rest, leaning against the side of some building that lined the alleyway Songas had transported them to.

"What am I going to do, Songas? My purpose was founded upon a lie. I have destroyed my soul."

"Fix it."

How could he fix it? Fixing it was much easier said than done; Tarias could not even secure his mind, let alone his soul.

"You just try to make it right. Try to right your wrongs, however many that you have."

Even though it was a warm night in Aigerua, Tarias's skin was covered with goosebumps, and he shivered with cold. His skin was a gradient of purple, yellow, and beige bruises. Every little movement reminded him of the beatings he had endured just moments ago, but he was bandaged. He stared at the bandages with wonder.

"You wanted to torture me at one point. Why aren't you doing so now?"

Songas grinned. "Your superior ordered your death, yet you wish to justify it. You would die before you went against your superior. We need to dig you out of the grave your loyalty has buried you in."

The elf pulled Tarias up over his shoulder once more. Songas's tired legs would every so often buckle under the weight of carrying the injured elf. Tarias did not know their destination, but he knew he was in the Blue Aucs. It was calm here at this time of night, unlike the Yellow Aucs, where reveling ran rampant; however, there were still people in the restaurants having drinks. They were the affluent Sealandesq, and Songas, with his olive-tan skin, stuck out like a sore thumb. Once the two made it into a more residential part of Aucs, Songas stopped in his tracks. He stood there with closed eyes and looked as if he were listening for something. He slowly wandered to the shut door of one of the many homes in the area. He knocked on the door, and an elderly elf came to the door. His skin was beige, and he had a thick white beard that stretched down. His face was scarred and one of his ears was mangled with hematoma lumps, yet his smile was warm and welcoming.

"Oh! What have we here?" asked the elderly elf.

"My friend here is injured. I only ask for a place to sleep for the night."

The elderly elf looked Songas up and down. "A Midlandesq elf being friends with a Sealandesq elf? That is not a common sight, especially in this day and age."

"My name is Andlaur," said the elf with an extended hand.

Songas shook it. "I am Songas."

The elderly elf looked around his home with disappointment. "I apologize. I do not have any room inside my own home—my family is here—but I do have space in my storehouse, if you would not mind. I will bring you items to make your rest more comfortable."

Songas smiled. "Anything with a roof will suffice. I thank you greatly for your hospitality and kindness."

Andlaur bowed. "It is my duty."

CHAPTER 10

It took Tarias a week to recover enough strength to do basic, everyday actions; and during this recovery, he witnessed Songas's kindness. To repay Andlaur for his hospitality, Songas would venture out to the markets and buy food with his own money. If there was an issue in the home, Songas would be the first to offer his hand in aid, so long as it was not a personal matter of the family. Tarias watched from afar because his legs did not permit him to move. He was affixed to the floor at this point, forced to reflect on his past. The children were afraid of him, almost like they knew what he had done; but they looked toward Songas with admiration, longing to be just like him. Tarias could see it in their eyes.

Every day, he tried to crawl his weight back over his legs until he finally obtained enough strength to keep himself up. His legs shook under him like the hollow bones of a bird if they were put under the weight of a horse. He was forced to lean on the wall while he journeyed from the floor to the shed door that was only a leg away. Usually, Songas would lift him up and into Andlaur's home so he would not suffer loneliness, but Tarias beat him to it. He stumbled through the door to the family having their breakfast. They stared at him with awe. He spotted a bit of loose straw on the floor. He looked around, and his eyes fell onto a broom. He stumbled toward it like he was entranced. His hands grabbed the broomstick and went to sweep up the straw off the floor.

"No need, Tarias! Please sit down and recover," said Andlaur as he stood up to intercept Tarias's act.

Tarias looked down at the floorboards to hide his eyes. "Please, sir, allow me to help but a bit."

The elderly elf's hand still reached out with pity, but he halted his grasp. He nodded and went back to the dining table.

"Well, you can do that after you eat, lad."

Andlaur pulled a seat out next to him. Tarias grinned with joy while Andlaur reached out to grab him and help carry Tarias's weight. Tarias, despite wishing to walk himself, allowed his aid. He set his weight down on the chair. The elderly elf sat next to another elf, about the same age as Tarias, who looked to be a younger clone of Andlaur's; and to that elf's side, there was a Sealandesq elfe, also about the same age as Tarias, who held a baby in her arms. Two other children were seated at the table, smiling at their mother. He stared at them with sad longing, but his prolonged stare caught the attention of one of the children, who returned him a pout.

Look away. You are frightening the child, sounded in Tarias's head, in his own voice.

Tarias spun his head around in confusion, but soon his eyes fell over Songas's, he understood why that thought had arrived. Tarias nodded to the Esku. He thanked Songas in his head with the knowledge that Songas would be listening to his thoughts. Tarias was not used to it, but because he could not prevent it, he figured it was futile to resist.

It was a quiet breakfast. The children were well-behaved; they never interrupted their elders and listened to their parents. Andlaur seemed to command respect amongst the family. His son listened with full attention to his words, and whenever Andlaur spoke to his grandchildren directly, they too listened with the same full attention. He was truly the elf of the house. He and Songas would joke over trivial topics like the strange characters at the local bathhouse or how brutal the rain had been recently, but he never spoke about past wars, despite the sword that hung over the fireplace's mantelpiece. Tarias noticed Andlaur had one fewer finger than usual on his right hand, and it was his pointer finger. He felt compelled to ask about it, but Songas looked at Tarias with wide eyes as if he was imploring him not to.

Andlaur never asked Tarias what had happened to him. He took the soul seeker in and fed him without any questions, for this was the Terukian way. A good Terukian helped their countryelves without debating it; but what was strange was how Songas, a Midlandesq elf, was so willing to help Andlaur and his family. Songas stood up.

"I want to thank you and your family, Andlaur, for your grace. Tarias would not have been able to recover as well as he has without your aid. Please accept this bag of coin as a token of gratitude." Songas pulled a sack of gold from his robe and extended it to Andlaur.

Andlaur stared at the coin with awe. "I cannot. I really cannot accept all this gold. This is far too much! I am not worthy of it."

Songas smiled. "I insist. You deserve it. Use it toward something important."

Tears fell from Andlaur's eyes. He shot up and hugged Songas. He squeezed the elf with an almost excessive amount of strength while his tears continued to wet his cheeks.

"You truly do not know how much this means to me, Songas. You have been a blessing to our family."

"It is my pleasure, Andlaur."

Songas went to lift Tarias up.

"You may stay longer! That Tarias looks like he could use at least another day."

"Oh no, it is alright! We must get going anyway. Thank you, Andlaur." Songas bowed to the old elf.

Tarias and Songas left Andlaur's home. The streets were especially busy. Tarias attempted to climb down the steps that led to Andlaur's door, but his legs were still shaky from his wounds, so Songas came to his aid by slinging his arm for a moment under Tarias's shoulder. They kept close while they walked the streets. Songas's eyes gazed forward, but Tarias kept his gaze wandering about, so he could see everyone in view. He did not understand why Songas was so content with being unaware of his surroundings.

"Why are you not keeping an eye on all the strangers?"

"I am doing something better. I know when one holds the thought of striking me, and the thought always comes before the action."

This made sense to Tarias, but Songas was still a strange elf to him.

"Why did you give the old elf so much coin?"

Songas opened his mouth, but words did not come out. He looked down.

"You probably thought that Andlaur's son was the father of those children."

"Of course."

"He is not. He is their uncle. I killed Andlaur's son."

"Was it a mistake?"

"No."

"Then why do you feel bad? It was what you were supposed to do. It was your job."

"You keep having thoughts like that. This is why you don't have peace in your head. Your soul is rejecting those thoughts, yet you keep forcing them upon it. Andlaur does not work. He was a soldier, and despite being gifted a home as a reward for his service, he does not have the health to work. His other son does not make enough to provide for them. He is in debt, and if he does not pay, he would lose a hand. The elf I killed was the provider for their whole family. Yes, he was an insurgent, but his death caused pain to innocents. I struggle to live knowing that I have destroyed families, so I do everything in my power to make sure they are provided for."

These words stung Tarias like a jagged knife. He wished he did not feel the same way—it would have made his life far easier—but the pain still stung him. Tarias did not know how many people he had harmed in his line of work. He had killed people, *many* people, so frequently that his heart had grown accustomed to the discomfort it brought him. He forgot that it was pain he felt, for the pain was so normal and constant that it became invisible to him. What is noticed first, change or constancy?

"I can only be absent from the Koroark's side for so long," Songas said. "I must go back, but I cannot leave until I know who your superior is."

Tarias attempted to convince himself one last time. He did not wish to betray everything he had stood for until now, but the burning magma in his gut and throat forced him to speak.

"The elf in the black mask."

Songas swore under his breath. He paced back and forth until he grabbed Tarias by the sides of his head and squeezed.

"If you wish to right your wrongs, fix *this*."

He released his grasp on Tarias's skull and walked off into the crowd of people. As he ventured deeper into the crowd, others overlapped him, blocking his figure from view, until eventually a faint puff of smoke wisped away from the middle of the mob of elves. Tarias stood in the streets of the Blue Aucs, directionless.

Tarias did not know how he would fix his chaotic mind. Every angry voice in his head ordered him to return to the house he stayed at. Perhaps Ederra could help him; but only if she was truly loyal, and not a plant from the black-masked elf.

It was the only idea he had. He was a shambling mess, and he walked like he had just crawled up from a grave. His legs could not keep him straight—they buckled over each other, sending him side-to-side, bumping into people while he traveled forward.

The walk there was long, and his legs ached with unavoidable pain. As he walked, he caught stares from others as if he was a foreigner, despite him still being in the Blue Aucs. He wondered why; he had never received looks like that before. In the distance, the Golden Statue of Ee'nak stood with the same pride that the Terukians around Tarias had. He walked to its side and rested his hands on the ledge that kept the water inside the fountain under the statue. He gazed down at his reflection, and he saw that his face was covered with swollen purple-yellow bruises. Their pain finally began to sting when he pressed on the lumps that covered his face. His instinct upon seeing his reflection was not to recoil back in fear, but to stare at himself longer than he ever had before. He felt like he needed to, like he *had* to. It was a necessary action for his atonement.

He took his feet away from the water. Knowing that he would now have more attention on him because of his proximity to the Palace, he kept his depressed and sunken eyes down to watch his surroundings. Tarias did not take his usual route, as he figured that the prying eyes of whatever other elves the black-masked elf had at his disposal would be searching keenly for his return.

The house stood off in the distance, and the door was wide open.

Strange, Tarias thought.

But everything up to that point had been strange. He walked down the road in front of the door and peered into the building. No light from torches or candles flickered out of the doors or windows. Ederra must not have been present. She always kept a candle lit in the main room. He trudged towards the front door and stepped into the house.

There was nothing inside. No chairs, cabinets, paintings, or any other furnishings. Tarias stuck his hand out for his room's door handle and entered. His bed and wardrobe were gone, but the mirror still stood in the corner.

CHAPTER 11

The mirror was the only piece of furniture in the house. Tarias remembered the last time he had seen it. He had left it turned around so that he would not see his reflection, but it was returned to its original orientation. Was this to *taunt* him?

He wondered why his appearance did not give him the same unstable heartbeat as it did the last time he looked at it. It could have been his tarnished appearance, devoid of any perceived beauty, that led to this change. His sins were left unhidden, uncovered by his appearance. He was unmasked, and he was surprised by what he saw. He inched forward to the mirror, and his hands grazed his chin. He uncovered his torso, and his robes fell to his sides, resting from his waist where they were tightly bound.

Unconsciously, Tarias recoiled backwards. Countless bandaged gashes and bruises covered his entire body. He had not noticed them when he was resting, but his entire body was in pain, and now the image of him *hurt* was seared into his mind. He had always won until now.

The door creaked. Tarias spun around to a knife lunging toward his gut. He spun back, grabbed the wrist that held the knife, and hooked his arm under the shoulder of his attacker. He slammed them into the wall and sent his fist into the middle of their torso. Their other arm reached for their abdomen, and Tarias felt them crumbling down to the floor as they dropped their knife onto the ground. Tarias stomped his foot on the knife and kicked it backward.

"Ederra?"

Tarias stepped away. Ederra was dressed in a lackluster gray dress, and she was still regaining her composure.

"So, you were never *my* servant. You were here to spy on me."

Ederra coughed. "You are wrong, Tarias. I was indeed under your command, but you betrayed us. This had to be done."

Tarias felt capable of focusing for the first time since he had killed Elreina. He crouched down and grabbed the knife from under him. Ederra began to rise. Tarias pushed her and grabbed her by the nape of her neck while he led her out of his room. He came to see that the door that led into the house was now closed.

"I imagine you are new to this profession," Tarias said.

Ederra glared at Tarias. Tarias pulled her down and forced her to sit down on one of the living room chairs. He took a seat.

"Is this your first task?" asked Tarias while he grew comfortable in his chair.

Ederra did not speak. Tarias pointed to the door.

"This type of job is truly sink or swim. You should have left that door open. I am a wanted Sealandesq fugitive, and you are a pretty Midlandesq elfe. That door was your way out, in case you failed."

"I did not plan to fail."

"You did not plan. Where and when did the black-masked elf give you the order to kill me?"

Again, Ederra did not speak.

"You are not cut out for this, Ederra. You are too kind. If this is your first task, you truly do not know what you are getting into."

Tarias gestured around the room.

"I should have known you were the one to move that mirror back into its original spot. You were the only one who knew of my panics, or at least the only one to know their trigger. That was pretty ingenious. You thought it would be easy to kill me in a state of despair."

Ederra looked away to the door, frowning.

"Ederra. You have a kind heart. You do not wish to go down the same path as me. You will suffer the same despair I suffer. Do you truly wish for that?"

She spun her head towards Tarias. "He *saved* me!"

"From what? He only brought you from one sector of damnation to another. He is no savior. He will use you and discard you as he did me."

"You threw out his grace! You betrayed him by colluding with insurgents! You have mocked him when he gave you this home, when he gave you me!"

Ederra rose up and lunged at Tarias. He rolled out of his chair and tackled her to the ground. She fumbled back and Tarias pinned her down.

"Please, you do not wish for this life. You are clouded by his false words. *He* is the insurgent. Please do not relegate your life to this."

Tarias stood up and wrapped his robes around him once more while he left the room. To his surprise, Ederra did not run after him. He felt better about himself after he had talked to her; he felt like his words were *true*. It was strange speaking about the black-masked elf in that manner. He was by no means calm, but his heartbeat became a bit more relaxed, and his thoughts, once a hurricane of worry and anguish, were now more of an angry storm. He fumed at the thought of the lies the black-masked elf had told him. His head was now a boiling pot ready to spill its contents on those who wronged him.

The only clue of where the black-masked elf stayed was where he had stood on the mound in the throne room. He remembered that he stood to the left of the Koroark on the mound. Was he his guard, or did he hold even more significance? Tarias had never been told why the elf wore a black mask, and he had never asked, because he always told himself that he should not be concerned about it. But he *should* have been concerned about it.

Not knowing where to go, Tarias did what he did best: nothing. He waited until Ederra grew tired of sitting in her failure. It was not long until she left the house with a bitter look on her pretty face. Tarias wondered what had drawn her to a profession like this. Combat was not the kindest to one's looks; but then again, her looks might've been enough to prevent someone from trying to beat her in combat.

However, it was not enough to prevent her from being tailed. She left through the front in little time and hurried down the middle of the road. Her feet kicked off the ground like she was in a desperate hurry, so Tarias followed her with the same desperation. It was not quite a chase, for it was more like a gentle stroll with each individual yards apart. She turned her head side-to-side while she walked—it must have been her best attempt to keep aware of her surroundings. Tarias stayed on the fringe of the road, but because the middle of the road was less dense, Ederra moved far more quickly than Tarias.

He walked past a clothier's table and snagged a cloth hood. After wrapping the hood around his head, he for the first time deliberately stepped into the Midlandesq's section of the street. There were enough elves in the streets to allow him some concealment, but there were far fewer elves there than on the narrow sides where azkozals were hitched and where merchants peddled their wares. He adjusted his speed to a more comfortable one to keep him at a distance from Ederra.

She walked deeper into the Green Aucs. With the subtlety of a big cat staring down prey, Tarias kept himself deep within the jungle of the people on the road. As they ventured further into the Green, the sides where Sealandesq elves traveled became less and less dense, for few Sealandesq elves had the coffers to even spend only part of the day in the depths of the Green. Tarias felt like he was being watched at this point. He felt like he was not supposed to be there, and soon enough, the Midlandesq elves would catch on to him. He tried his best to feign their mannerisms: their pompous gait and their excessively proud hands. They took up space, and they did not care if they got in the way of another. They walked and talked like they were never told 'no'. They held no concern for their surroundings, for they had a naïve understanding of society. Tarias knew they felt safe.

Ederra's worried actions transformed into this same feeling of being at ease. Tarias noticed this about the Midlandesq elves in the Green Aucs: they always seemed to be at home, and everyone seemed to be a *friend*.

"You there!" an elf voice yelled behind Tarias.

There was an anxiety that followed every Sealandesq elf in the Green Aucs, and Tarias tried his hardest to suppress it.

He strutted toward the side of the road where the Sealandesq elves traveled, but the clattering of steel plates seemed to hurry faster and faster over to him. The clattering came closer, closer, and even closer, until they could not have been more than a foot away from him.

When he had the feeling a hand lingered over his shoulder, he stood still and stuck his foot out, sending one of the guards down. The other guard went to draw his bludgeon—they did not carry blades in the Green Aucs—but before he could swing, he joined his comrade in eating the hard street bricks.

Tarias ran before he could see if he had gained an audience. Undoubtedly, this would have spooked Ederra, so he ran to the alleyways and sent his hands to the side of a brick wall. After scaling it, he planted his feet on the rooftop and ran for one of the taller buildings in the Green Aucs. He sat. He watched the streets for Ederra. His eyes followed the road she had been traveling down with the hope of spotting her once more; and spot her he did. She rushed for one of the buildings in the Green Aucs's town square. She loitered like a sad child searching for a lost puppy until the elf with the black mask grabbed her by the elbow.

He hooked her elbow with his own and walked down the streets. Again, Tarias could not decipher his emotions, especially when such a long distance separated the two of them. He never shook his head 'yes' or 'no'; and even if he did give some sort of gesture, he would do it in such a subtle manner that it would've been almost invisible a yard away, let alone with several buildings spanning the distance between them.

Tarias stood up and stepped his foot forward, but he soon retracted it with a fear-filled hesitation. He reeked with angst at the thought of fighting the black masked elf. He convinced himself to step forward once more while his knees trembled with timidity. His thoughts were a little clearer at this moment. He knew he had to question the elf, but he could not convince himself that he was prepared to do so. He had seen him fight only once before, and the duel he witnessed so long ago was a flicker in his mind. The elf was *fast*, and Tarias was unsure if he could keep up with his speed.

Tarias's worries made the world slow down, and it moved slowly enough for him to notice the particles of black dust manifesting in front of his eyes. He shot his arm to grab one of the clay tiles that composed the roof below him and swung it in front of him. It slammed into the face of the elf in the black mask. His mask was knocked to the side and sent it down to the ground. Tarias's heart raced with excitement—he would finally see the face of the elf with the black mask—but when he turned around, he saw nothing but a black void where his face should have been.

Tarias blinked. The elf was gone.

"What?"

Immediately after Tarias had spoken, the elf in the black mask manifested in front of him. He shot his arm down and slammed it forward. The elf stomped on his Tarias's foot, sending him stumbling backward, but this could not stop the roof tile from slamming into the elf's knee.

The two fell and rolled down the sides of the building. Tarias landed on one side, and the elf in the black mask landed on the other. Tarias's back slammed into the brick below. The air was stolen from him, and he hit his head with such force he was shocked he was still aware of his surroundings. He dragged himself up by climbing up the crates that lined the road.

The elf with the black mask limped with what Tarias assumed to be murder in his eyes. He had his blade drawn and pointed at Tarias. Tarias, unarmed, scrambled around trying to find something to defend himself with. Nothing but sand rested beneath his feet, so he kicked it in the face of the masked elf. It only blurred the elf's vision for a moment, for his mask halted the sand particles from harassing his eyes. Tarias tackled the elf to the ground, and the masked elf dropped his blade; it bounced twice before it rested on the brick-paved ground.

Tarias had no time to thank the Koroark for his luck. He pinned the elf's shoulders to the ground and grabbed the masked elf's left wrist. While he kept the wrist pinned to the ground, Tarias dug his other arm under the elf's pinned arm and grabbed his own wrist. He lifted the masked elf's elbow and dragged the elf's pinned arm across the ground, down toward his waist. Tarias hurried to rip and twist the elf's sword arm out of its socket.

The masked elf sent his hips up toward his sword arm, rolling Tarias onto his back.

"*Fuck.*"

The masked elf hammered his fists into Tarias's face. While the elf loaded for another punch, Tarias kicked one of his legs up, forcing the elf to stick his hands out to stop himself from tumbling over. He shot his hips up again, and when the masked elf gave him the *smallest* bit of room, Tarias brought his legs in between them and kicked the masked elf off of him. He rolled to his side and then to his feet, propelled by the will to *stay alive*. At the same time, the masked elf got up, but Tarias lifted his knee and sent his foot into the elf's gut. He staggered backward to the wall and Tarias rushed him. The elf raised his hands to protect his face, so Tarias sent a knee to his body instead. His knee landed in the elf's lamellar armor, and it would have stung were it not for the adrenaline pumping throughout Tarias's body. One hook, no, two hooks struck the sides of the masked elf's face in quick succession.

Tarias reached for the elf's mask and tried to lift it, but the elf surprisingly still had the strength and energy to push Tarias away. Before Tarias could regain his posture, the masked elf grabbed the handle of his sword that rested on the floor.

He lifted it up, but there was no blade to cut Tarias with— at least, not until particles seemed to appear from thin air. They floated, hovering in the air like the black particles that came about with displacement, but they were *clear*. The only reason Tarias noticed them was because they seemed to bend light like little beads of glass. They coalesced together to form the blade, and the blade took on its silvery steel luster. At first, it was translucent; but eventually, the beads gave it a fullness that made it opaque.

Tarias blinked again, and he saw the masked elf reaching for the handle he had dropped. A wooden board leaned against the side of one of the buildings next to Tarias. He grabbed the board and rushed for the masked elf while his blade manifested. He slammed it toward the elf's head. The masked elf raised his blade, probably with the hope it would manifest in time, but the wooden plank knocked the particles away and slammed into the side of the mask. The mask cracked and a piece of its jaw fell to the ground, leaving the elf's chin and left eye visible to Tarias. The concussive force of the strike forced the elf's hand to let go of his handle, dropping it to the floor.

Tarias reached for the rest of the mask to rip it off of the elf's face, but the elf's body blew away into the wind, the exposed half of his face contorted with obvious rage. After the elf disappeared, Tarias grabbed the jaw and blade in both of his palms.

CHAPTER 12

His fight with the masked elf had drawn attention from all the elves in the Green Aucs, but his escape was swift; for, compared to the average guard, Tarias outclassed them in speed. He jumped over barrels, vaulted over stalls, slid under fences, and threaded through the large crowds of Midlandesq elves.

Once he had finally made it away from the guards that pursued him, he perched himself on top of a random building within the Yellow Aucs. He laid the two items, the jaw and sword handle, out in front of him.

He first held the jaw in his hands. He had seen it countless times before, but now he could get a closer look, a closer *feel* of it. It felt to be made of some polished stone. The surface felt like marble, but it held no shine. Its black surface absorbed the light around it, and, even further, it felt as though it was beginning to absorb the strength from Tarias's *hands.* Afraid of letting it take any more from him, he gently placed the jaw down on the roof of the building. His hands strayed from it and reached for the sword handle. He recognized the design, but it looked to be stripped from an old painting or mosaic from long ago, for its design was not one common amongst any soldier in recent times. Its hilt was shaped like a hook and swooped toward the knuckles; or at least he assumed it swooped toward the knuckles, as it felt more natural in the hand that way. He could not say he knew for certain if he held it in the correct orientation, but the way one quillon curved up and one curved down implied that the downward side held the edge of the blade. It had a similar *draining* feeling as the black mask, but it was far more muted in comparison.

He had to find Songas. Tarias had no direction, no thought, nor even a hunch of where to go. He climbed down the building and walked away. He figured he would wander around the Yellow Aucs first, in case Songas were there, and simply think of the Esku's name in his head. He did so, but it came to no avail; however, he was not disappointed, for he did not truly expect the Midlandesq elf to be present in the shithole that was the Yellow Aucs. His wander into the Blue led to a similar outcome. Nothing interesting occurred, but, again, he did not expect the Midlandesq elf to be present in such a Sealandesq-dominant district.

He then came back to the Green Aucs. He refused to cross through to the Black Aucs to the north. The Green Aucs was safer than the Black. It was dominated by the Midlandesq, but they were far more open to their Sealandesq *pets*. He did not think of the Esku's name in this district, for he knew the risk of attracting unwanted attention from other soul seekers was higher in this district.

Finally, he made it to the Red Aucs. The Red Aucs was calm and quaint. It could be described as the most tolerant of the Aucs. It was the only district foreigners were allowed to visit, but rarely were they ever seen. In his lifetime, Tarias had only ever seen one 'man' in the Red Aucs. It was a strange sight: his ears were rounded as if they were trimmed and rolled over when he was young, and he had curly hairs extending down from his jaw. The other foreigners were more normal folk, like the occasional Jutian stubman or a Sombraski elf. Okrs were a rare sight—they did not like others—but their diplomats often visited the Red. He thought of Songas's name, and he continued to do so until a voice sounded in his head.

Forward.

Tarias nodded and walked forward. In front of him stood a bathhouse. It was large and had two signs: the one that pointed left read 'Terukians', and the one that pointed right read 'Others'.

Right.

Tarias thought it strange that Songas wished for him to enter with the foreigners, but he did not wish to question it. He stepped in, and he was met with a large number of Sombraski elves, darker-skinned elves with charcoal-toned skin. Songas sat in their midst. They were not the only folk around—an okr or two could be spotted—but they made up the overwhelming majority. Tarias removed his garments, while tucking the handle and jaw securely within his robes, and joined Songas in the bath.

I beat him, thought Tarias.

You did, said the same voice in Tarias's head.

Tarias opened his eyes and stared at Songas, and Songas returned his stare.

"You are thinking far more clearly, Tarias, now that you are on your path of atonement."

"Are you inspecting my head for any other things I am guilty of?"

"Unfortunately."

A smile cracked on Tarias's face.

"You truly have beat him. Before you came here, I heard word of it. The Koroark knew upon his arrival. He read the elf's mind. You *seared* defeat into his mind, and he is going to seek your death."

"Something he already had done. It is nothing I cannot deal with."

"You have dealt with it before, but you have changed something within him. I felt what you had done. His head is a muddied mess of rage. But your victory was a fluke, with what I know about you thus far."

"You do know quite a bit," Tarias said.

"Nevertheless, he must have seen something within you that made you worth his time. Did you notice anything strange when you fought him?"

The memory of the masked elf appearing before him resurfaced in his mind, and the thought of the elf's blade manifesting followed.

"Ah, I see. There is something special about you, after all."

Tarias's world faded to black. There was mist below his bare feet, and he was dressed in his gray robes. In the fog before him, Songas emerged. He wore a red jant, and between them on the floor lay the handle and black jaw.

"Either you can see the future, or you can reverse time. Both are frightening abilities. It is time you figure out what you can do with your newly calm mind. Pick up the black jaw."

Tarias did what the Esku said. He felt his strength drain away.

"That mask is made of ieomolb. It will drain you of your strength. Throw it out."

Tarias clutched the mask in his hands and looked off into the haze that surrounded him. He raised his hand to chuck the fragment, but his hand gripped it *tighter*. He felt his arms drop down in front of him and he frowned at the jaw.

"Do not look at the mask with longing for what could have been. You have been betrayed. Cut your past away with a hot blade."

Tarias's grip became even tighter, yet he turned and launched the jaw into the deep mist. He returned his eyes to Songas and gazed at the handle. Songas nodded, so Tarias grabbed the handle and held it in his hands.

"If you are able to experience the future, then surely you will be able to do what I ask of you now. Bring the blade back."

Tarias looked down at the handle. He tried to focus on it, but he could not figure out what he was supposed to focus on. The mist around him turned into vicious winds while his head filled with more and more anxiety. Tarias felt a hand grip his forearm, and the air around him became less violent.

"All soul seekers have done things that they are not proud of. Every individual elf has done things they regret as well. Some actions fall in a range of greater severity, but what truly matters is your heart. If you thought what you did was the right thing, then you would have done it. If you knew Elreina was pregnant, would you have killed her?"

The winds returned. They shoved Tarias to each side, back and forth, sending the handle flying out of his hands and back to the black mist on the ground. The violence sent him to his knees, tears dripping from his eyes.

"*Yes.*"

Songas took a knee and slapped his hand on Tarias's shoulder. Tarias looked up, and he saw Songas's cocky smile on his face. *Why was he always smiling?* The Esku sat down with crossed legs and picked the blade up in his hands.

"It is interesting how soul seekers often recruit orphans. You, I, and almost every soul seeker I know is an orphan. Maybe it is because our lack of relatives could make us even more loyal to our nation and people, or maybe since our ranks are comprised of orphans, we are drawn to others like us; nonetheless, it is a fact that the majority of us are orphans. Parents are often where people receive their moral guidance, and without them, even though people may form their own moral code, they can easily make mistakes that can scar their souls. I once lived in an orphanage. I was alone and stuck in my thoughts. The other children thought I was strange, and they avoided me because I always seemed to know too much about them. I would know things that they had never told me. I did not understand that I had something different; I could *feel* what they thought in their heads. At one point, I ran away because I could not sleep with their chaotic dreams. About a week later, I was forced to return for food."

Songas paused.

"Do you remember the famine around ten years ago?"

Tarias nodded.

"For the longest time, I could not get the memory of it out of my head. The orphanage had stockpiled food, but I had just returned from starving. I went to the fringes of society, far away from anyone's thoughts, so that I might finally be delivered *peace*. I entered a building that housed minds far more disturbed. It did not help that I was already starving, and that the others had only begun their rations. I stockpiled the rations. I would slip extra rations underneath my robes and hide them in a hole in the wall. I amassed so much food I forgot how much I had. I took too much, because I felt like I needed it to survive. The other children's minds were filled with primal hunger, and they quickly turned against one another. A number… A number of the other children had passed away because of the starvation they endured. I felt their thoughts as they died. I felt their withering and wild thoughts. I couldn't take it anymore. They died, and it was because of *me*. I ran away once more, and eventually, I was found by an Esku."

The winds died down. Despite how guilty Songas had sounded while he told his story, he did not collapse. He kneeled with resolve, and his smiling eyes seemed to convey that he was not being dragged down by his past. Tarias, still sitting on his knees, looked up at the Esku.

"What gets you through the bad things you have done? What calms the roaring voices in your head?"

"I listen to the voices that tell me what I did was wrong, and I vow to never do such a thing again. Even further, I make it a point to live my life in a way that my actions will bring about a world where such things would not happen again. That experience formed me. It gave my life purpose. Your voices are beckoning you to yours."

CHAPTER 13

Reality faded back into Tarias's view. Songas, the Red Esku, returned to sitting down across from him in the bath. He arose while turning to keep his unclothed body from view. He grabbed a towel and went to a more private room to dry himself off. Tarias did the same. They dressed themselves and departed from the establishment. Songas led the way, as he always seemed to know exactly where he was going. He took Tarias down a long alleyway. It was hard to keep track of how many alleys there were in Aigerua, for the streets sprawled aimlessly. Each Aucs was like its own separate town.

There was an old tower that looked battered by weather. The green paint that decorated its bricks was being stripped away by the passing of time, and the door hung lopsided off its hinges. When Songas went to open the door, the end furthest from the hinges scraped along the ground. It was a blessing that not many people walked in this part of the Red Aucs, as the squeak that came from the door would have beckoned anyone's attention. They entered through cobwebs.

The ladder that climbed to the top of the tower looked to have fallen to the ground. The tower had a large footprint, but it would have been hard to believe from within as the room was filled to the brim with old crates and building materials. Songas walked towards the trapdoor and opened it. Beneath the now-opened trapdoor, there was a hole that tunneled down into a deep abyss. It looked to delve so deep into the ground that if one of them were to slip off the rungs of the ladder, the sound of their plummeting body would not be heard hitting the ground. Songas, taking the initiative, climbed down the ladder without worry or wonder. Tarias followed. The climb down was quiet and boring, and if Tarias had not feared the drop, he thought he would have fallen asleep midway.

Songas's feet tapped the bottom of the tunnel. Tarias heard the fumbling of limbs go about before he stepped his own two feet down. The sound of hard steel dropping on a wooden table rang throughout the chamber.

"Ah, finally," sighed Songas.

Sparks lit in the air, and soon, flames emitted from a small bowl of tinder. Songas grabbed a candle in his hand and lit it. Afterwards, he followed the perimeter of the room and lit several candlesticks that lined the walls. With the room now lit, Tarias could see what was contained within. Countless shelves with trinkets hung on the walls. There were three standing closets, and one of them had one of its doors crept slightly open, its contents overflowing. A floor cushion sat in the center of the circular room.

"You keep belongings?"

Songas grinned. "You don't?"

"Why would I? I can get whatever I wish as I go."

"That is an amazing skill to have, but do you not keep anything you like?"

Tarias shook his head. "I do not understand."

Songas raised a single finger into the air. He walked to one of the shelves, and his hand hovered around the trinkets until his grasp locked onto one that grabbed his attention. He went to Tarias and handed it over to him. It was a green ribbon with a wavy gold stitching adorning its hems.

"I stole this from a girl," said Songas with a smile.

Tarias stared at the ribbon. "Why?"

"Because! She was stressed about an event she was preparing to attend, and she was nitpicking every single thing about her fashion before traveling. I wanted to put her at ease, so I stole this ribbon. She scoured *everywhere* for a replacement. I told her she would find one, and that she would not have to stress about such a small thing. She eventually did, to no one's surprise, and I kept the ribbon for a laugh whenever I had downtime. Do you not have memories like this?"

Tarias sat down and stared at the ground with deep thought. It looked like his eyes were hammering into the ground. He looked up to Songas with eyes that reflected his empty thoughts.

"No," he said. "I try not to remember things."

"Well, start remembering things. Remember the fond times in your life. They truly do make the hard times easier to get through."

Songas walked to one of his closets and opened it. Afterward, he turned to Tarias with an open hand. Tarias reached for where he kept the black jaw and sword handle, and Songas nodded with affirmation. He gave the Red Esku the two items.

"I will keep this black jaw as evidence, but I will not be able to bring it to the Koroark anytime soon."

Tarias shook his head. "Why not?"

"It has to do with who the elf in the black mask is. It would be far too grand of an accusation to bring forward. The proof cannot be a simple jaw—it must be a blatant act of rebellion."

"Who is the elf in the black mask?"

Songas shook his head. "I think you know quite intimately that is not a question I can answer."

Songas closed his eyes, but Tarias felt like he was peering into his soul. Songas opened his eyes.

"You know things. Ask another question."

Tarias thought hard. He looked around the room as if it were filling with his memories. He rarely ever saw the elf in the black mask with other people. Usually, he appeared for but a small moment to give Tarias a task.

"There have been many substantial events in recent times. Think."

Tarias thought harder. Everything he had done in the past few weeks replayed in his head. He thought of the elf's face being a blackened void. He shook his head. The memories of Ederra and the black-masked elf came to the forefront of his head, but Ederra was just another Midlandesq elfe. It would have been unlikely for her to know anything. At last, the most impactful day of Tarias's life thus far pierced his thoughts. It was uncomfortable to replay the events in his head, but he was taken back to the black-masked elf stopping Yodoa at the steps of the palace. *Why was he there?* After, the memory of the masked elf standing on the mound crept forth. *Why was he on the mound with the Koroark, Princess Elreina, and the Koroark's brother?*

"The mound is sacred, is it not? Only certain people may step on it. The Koroark was at the top, and his brother stood midway. The black masked elf was on the opposite side, but he was slightly lower than the brother of the Emperor. Who may step on the mound?"

"Only individuals permitted to do so by the Koroark."

"Do these individuals have a common characteristic?"

Songas looked down. "They are most often family."

Tarias shook his head. "This cannot be. The Koroark has no son. Princess Elreina was his only child."

"An elf may have other family than his children, no?"

"His brother… Nakneir… Does he have a son?"

Songas did not respond immediately. He bent over and pulled the cushion back to him, then placed the two items in the center of the room. He knelt on the cushion, closed his eyes, and tilted his head to the ground.

"Yes. Yes, he does."

"What is his son's name?"

"Adoneir."

Tarias stepped back. The elf in the black mask's name was *Adoneir*. He struggled to even shift his gaze. All of the soul seeker's focus was on the nephew of the Koroark. The room grew cooler, which was strange, as it was already cool due to being so deep below the surface. Tarias turned his head to Songas, who at that moment had manifested the blade.

"This is a very significant weapon, Tarias. Do you remember the tale of Adoavi?"

"Of course. It is a tale of heroism."

Songas held the blade in his hands with his palms open. The blade end rested in his palm as if it were tangible and not brought from thin air. It still held a translucent ghostlike glow, yet Tarias now only noticed that it also had red splotches on the edge of its blade.

"Is this… Is this Adoavi's sword?"

"It is. Now, it is not necessary for you to use this sword, but it is necessary for you to have the skill to summon it. You can swing this sword for a hundred swings; no, thousands;

no, even for eternity, and it will *never* dull. Despite that, the sword is honestly useless."

The blade dissipated, and only the handle was left. Songas stood up and placed the handle on an empty shelf. Afterwards, he returned to kneel on his cushion. Tarias walked over to the ladder that led down to the room, and he looked up the tall tunnel to see the light from the open trap door.

"What was the purpose of this place? It looks like a forgotten hole."

"It *is* a forgotten hole. It was used for storage. I do not know exactly what for, but it was likely something that needed a temperate place. I found it in a much more decrepit state, and now it is my home. I have made it *mine*."

Tarias shook his head. The repetition of this concept of possession annoyed him. He walked over to the shelf that Songas placed the handle on and reached for it. He spun it around in his hands, examining every tiny bit of it.

"Do you know anything about the whereabouts of Adoneir? What his hobbies are, or anything regarding his daily routine?"

"For the safety of the royal family, I am bound by oath to not tell anyone of their daily happenings; however, there will soon be a holy day, as you should know."

Wonderful. A holy day would be the perfect event for Tarias to seek out Adoneir. He was of the royal and immortal line of Elreineir, and now that Elreina was dead, Adoneir was one of the possible heirs to the mound. Tarias, for the first time in a long time, had a smile on his face. He once more had a goal, a task, a *purpose.*

"Tarias, I will not be able to aid you in this. I cannot draw a blade to another Esku without the approval of the Koroark unless the Esku is actively attacking him."

Tarias nodded his head. He did not often question the word of others, especially not when said with such an official tone. His brain, by nature or by compulsion, led him to accept the rules of others.

"I would have expected it," Tarias said. "Adoneir will, without a doubt, be there watching for me. After I last saw him, he would want my head for besting him. The holiday must be the Cloth Festival. I will see him there."

Tarias turned around with an arm extended, reaching for the ladder. The room was already quiet, but a deafening *stop* sounded in his head. It echoed throughout his skull. Tarias clenched his aching head and spun around to meet Songas.

"You could have simply said it."

"I wanted you to experience once more the difference in ability between me, an Esku, and you, a *pretend* soul seeker. It is substantial. Yes, you have bested me, *once*—and yes, you have bested the elf in the black mask, *once*. I am telling you this as someone with experience: you will not beat him again. He knows your trick, yet you do not."

Tarias sat down and crossed his legs in front of the Red Esku. He leaned back with his arms posted out behind him.

"Well then, what do you want me to do?"

Songas's eyes opened, and the same sly smirk was painted on his face.

"I will make you a soul seeker."

CHAPTER 14

Songas was a very strange elf. He was not the tidiest person, but he still made sure things were put away somewhere; although, these items were not always stored in their proper locations. He would often put things that were not books on bookshelves, things that were not clothes in closets, and things that were not rugs on the floor.

How could this elf be a more proper soul seeker than Tarias? If Songas were anyone else, he would have found it laughable to say that this was a skilled assassin, for his home was left as an unkempt pit. Yes, the items within were put away, but everything was out of line and out of tune with how they were supposed to be.

Songas ate a pome fruit, and once he finished, he thankfully tossed the core into a bucket with other forms of garbage. Tarias could imagine himself letting out a relieved sigh, but he thought it improper to make his feelings known to the Midlandesq elf.

"You can quit your judgment, Tarias."

Tarias perked up. He grinned with humor, for he knew he should have expected Songas to read his thoughts by now.

"I have never seen an elf live like you," Tarias said.

"You have never seen anyone *live*. Yes, you know how to wear a mask and fake as if you know how someone is to act, but you have never yourself *lived*. You made yourself a drone, and by consequence, you lack a mind capable of nuance. Do you wish to understand your ability?"

Tarias stared at Songas with wide, desperate eyes.

"I do."

"You need the ability to see nuance for that. Remove any thought of how the world *ought* to be. Just sit back and see how it truly is."

Tarias shook his head. "Alright. I will try."

The two elves were kneeling face-to-face in the center of Songas's room. The Red Esku pulled a knife from his side. The knife was simple in its form, and the most elaborate marking it had was its 'maker's mark'. The Esku placed it down in between them and pointed at it with his index finger.

"What is this?"

Tarias chuckled. "It is a knife."

Songas smiled while he picked up the knife and twirled it around in his hands.

"What is it for?"

Tarias beckoned for Songas to hand him the knife, so Songas obliged. He looked at the blade's edge closely. It was made of worked iron and looked to have been recently polished. There was no sign of wear, but that could have just come down to it being put on a grindstone in the not-so-distant past. There were no serrations, so it must have been less made for sawing and more made for cutting. Only one side of the blade was sharpened, so stabbing with it was out of the question. Songas's smile widened. Why would he smile? Were his thoughts wrong?

"Why are you grinning?" Tarias asked.

"Continue your thoughts. It is interesting to witness your 'deductions'."

Tarias shook off the interruption and returned to discerning the blade's purpose. It was thinner than a typical blade, and its edge gradually curved up and peaked slightly behind the blade's spine. The soul seeker smiled with accomplishment.

"It is for skinning!"

Songas's usual grin reappeared. "No."

Tarias was taken aback. "What do you mean, no? It has all the characteristics of a skinning knife!"

Songas grabbed the knife from him. He walked over to a spot on the wall where a table rested. Several books stood stacked on top. He grabbed the top two books and placed them on the tabletop, revealing the third book. He grabbed that book and flipped through the pages until he found his desired page. His eyes lit up once he discovered it, and he stuck the knife's edge in between the covers and shut the book.

"Its thin blade makes it an amazing bookmark."

"Do you play jokes on me on purpose? You need to grow up, Songas."

"What joke? It is my bookmark. That is the purpose I purchased it for."

"It was made to skin. It was not made to keep track of where you were in your book."

"Did you ask the blacksmith yourself?"

He opened up the book once more and left it open on the page with the knife. Tarias took the knife from its pages, and he brought its blade close to his eyes. He held it so close that if Songas wanted to send it stabbing into his eyes, he could have.

"Where is this purpose of 'skinning'? I do not see it in the blade," Songas said.

Tarias sighed and placed his hand on his head. "Quit being childish, Songas."

"Childish, is it? I would not say so. You are missing something, Tarias."

"What am I missing?"

"The purpose of the knife is not innate within it, but rather found externally. Its purpose is defined by those who use it."

"That is stupid. It works best for skinning."

"It also works as a splendid bookmark."

"How does that not conflict with the blacksmith's intention?"

"Exactly! There is the beauty of it. The conflict."

Tarias sat dumbfounded. "Elaborate for me, Songas."

"Of course!"

Songas's happy, smiley face suddenly dried up into a cold glare.

"Your mind will never fully calm until you realize that you believe that you both should have and should *not* have killed Elreina."

At this point, Tarias felt an aching pain in his head. It seemed Songas could not stop himself from repeating contradictions.

"It was, at that time, what I thought to be a part of my purpose," Tarias said. "I now know that I had been led astray;

however, my purpose is *still* to act in the defense of the Koroark."

"But you are not a soul seeker. Where do you receive that purpose?"

Tarias's lips moved, but he could not speak. He did not have an answer for Songas. He sank into deep thought. Where did he receive his purpose?

"Yourself," Songas said.

"But why do I feel guilty for it?"

"Why do you feel the need to defend the Koroark?"

"I thought I was keeping the peace. I was supposed to make sure Terukian society was undisturbed by those who wished to bring others harm."

"Yet, you feel guilty."

"Why do I feel guilty?"

"Because you wish to keep the peace and to not bring others harm; yet you have brought harm to innocents."

"Yes. I have misacted. It is a natural thing, to make a mistake."

"Yet, if presented with the same situation, you said you would have killed Elreina once more. You would freely misact again? By your own volition?"

Songas always seemed to have a response to whatever Tarias said. It was annoying, but Tarias knew he meant well. What could Tarias have done? If it truly had been an order from his superior, ultimately from the Koroark, then he would have *had* to kill her. It would have been wrong not to.

"What would you say I do?" Tarias asked.

"Right your wrongs. Right them by actually fighting for the cause you have dedicated your heart to. You cannot be dedicated if your heart is not set to it."

Tarias shook his head.

"How am I supposed to set my heart right? I have committed atrocities, and they pain me every time I close my eyes. What salvation do I have?"

Songas walked over to one of the candles that lined the chamber walls and grabbed it. He strode over to the table with his newfound flame and grabbed one of the books. He held it high, and he brought the flame under.

"This is a written history of Teruk."

He set the book to flames. It erupted into a blazing ball in Songas's hand. Tarias's heart pounded like it was trying to break free from the prison bars that were his ribs. His hands were clenched like he wished to defend it, but the book was already aflame. Songas dropped it to the stone floor, leaving it to burn up into a mound of ash.

"Why would you do such a thing? Why would you burn a book?"

"How many atrocities were recorded in that book? Have you read it?"

"No. But that doesn't change the fact that you burnt knowledge."

"I have done something in the present to get rid of the past. You can do the same, Tarias, if you would only commit yourself to it."

How could he *burn away* the thought of killing a pregnant elfe when it permeated its roots so deeply within his mind? Every time he looked at his arms, he remembered the feeling of strangling the princess. It nestled in every thought, every memory, and he could tie it back to anything. If he thought of the Emperor, he thought of the princess. If he thought of an elfe, he thought of the princess. If he thought of a candle, he thought of the princess. He could not escape the thought of the princess. She haunted him like a pestering phantom. He could not rest. He could not think thoughts that did not relate to the princess. Even though she was dead and turned to stone, she seemed to have complete control over him. It humored Tarias a bit, but it scared him far more to know that he was not in control of his thoughts. He stood up.

"It is impossible. She has affected me in a manner that is far too severe to allow redemption. I am meant to be like this."

"She dwells in all corners of your mind. Stop running and confront her."

Tarias took a deep breath and nodded. What did he have to lose? He could barely function as a soul seeker given his current state. His mind was like a ball and chain, slowing him, weighing him down. The thought of reliving the murder sent chills down his spine, and it made his hands feel shaky like he was shivering from frigid air. While the memories of the event came pouring back into his view, his heart started to beat faster. He could feel his body begin to shake like an agitated child. His hands felt light and weak while his jaw chattered like a shivering dog left out in the rain.

An elfe in a green dress, adorned with gold cuffs and bracelets, stood in front of him. He only saw her. It was like he was staring down a deep tunnel where the only light was behind her. After having his vision stuck in the cement that was Elreina, he realized it was not light coming from behind her, but rather light coming *from* her. He reached his hand out, but it seemed to phase through her. He brought his hand around again, the light from her seemed to die down in its luminance. Her skin was soft. He felt the urge to grip it so that he could make sure she was *real*, but he recoiled his hand, frightened, like she was a poisonous ivy.

"You can't be real. I killed you…"

An olive-tan hand grabbed Tarias's arm. He looked up and saw Songas, now dressed again in his red robes, gripping his arm. Elreina came forward, but she did not have a bump where a baby could have been.

"Hello. Who are you?"

Tarias's teeth began to chatter once more.

"T—T—Tarias. I am Tarias. I am the elf who killed you. Are you alive?"

Songas shook his head.

"She is not. She is a memory of yours, and also a memory of mine. We are sharing this experience right now, but it is an experience in your head."

Songas placed his hand on Tarias's shoulder and stared into his eyes. Elreina stood with wonder like she knew nothing of what was happening before her.

"You know what you must do, Tarias," Songas said.

Tarias fell to his knees and bowed at Elreina's feet. His eyes scrunched up like they were battling tears from escaping. They twitched repeatedly, and his lips shuddered. The room was once again full of a black mist surrounding the three of them, and when his tears plummeted down, they fell through the misty ground.

"I am sorry. I killed you. I murdered your child in your womb. I have *wronged* you, for the *wrong* cause. You have now passed, and I know not how to fix this wound in my soul. I know not how to fix this sorrow and betrayal. I am *sorry.*"

Elreina lifted his chin up to see her face. "You did not know. You thought you were doing your duty. You believed that you were being led by your oath to my father, and by extension, your oath to me as his apparent successor. I forgive you, Tarias, but you must forgive yourself."

Elreina, like Songas, like Adoneir, and unlike Tarias, disappeared into a puff of smoke.

CHAPTER 15

The sullen expression left Tarias's face. His shoulders felt lighter. It was like Elreina's forgiveness had physically relieved him of some haunting burden, yet he still felt the lead that tugged behind him, hitched, restraining him. He beckoned for the sword handle, and Songas nodded, bringing it over to him.

"So, this is the great Adoavi's blade?"

"What is left of it."

Tarias closed his eyes. He thought of the blade. He thought of the blade manifesting from thin air. He tried to pull it from his memory the same way he had pulled Elreina. Particles, coming in the form of many tiny amorphous blobs, were pulled by some force to their respective destinations. Soon, a blade was in Tarias's hands.

"Where did the true blade go?" Tarias asked. "Weapons like this must be rare; it is the first time I have ever seen one."

"You are not currently seeing it. Open your eyes."

Tarias opened his eyes. After realizing what had just *not* happened, he sighed like a pouting child. He glared at the handle with a foul grimace while he gripped it with a simmering frustration.

"Do not be discouraged, Tarias. There is a reason why you can manifest it in your mind and not in front of you."

"It would be more helpful if I could bring it about in reality."

"Are your thoughts not reality?"

"No, that is absurd. There is only one reality."

"Yes, true. But your mind exists within that one reality, does it not?"

"Here you go again, Songas. You ask more and more philosophical questions. It is getting annoying."

"What else am I supposed to do in a room like this? Also, do not insult the method in which you have improved your skill in channeling."

"Do not tell me it has improved when I cannot bring about the sword."

"You have brought the sword into existence, not in your hands, but within your mind. This is the first step, Tarias. It is necessary to imagine what you wish to bring about in the world before you can bring it about. Will exists prior to action."

Tarias did not respond, for his frustration with his inability to bring the blade into existence consumed his thoughts. He had once worried about his murder of the princess; yet now that he had been forgiven, he stood exhausted by the thought of his ineptitude. He tossed the handle to the ground and looked up toward the ladder.

"What is the point? If I am having trouble learning this, I wonder how much of a struggle it would be to learn how to control what I experienced last I saw Adoneir."

"Why worry about the struggle? It is not going to aid you in getting any more adept at controlling it. Just practice."

Tarias stood up.

"*Sit down.*"

"Why?"

"I have saved you more than once. Have faith and simply listen. What harm can be done if you lose no matter what you do?"

Tarias sat back down.

"You are to meditate. Bring the blade to and fro in your mind, and soon, it will be your reality."

Tarias once more looked at the ladder.

"How long until the Cloth Festival?"

"Two and a half weeks."

Tarias fixed his legs into a proper kneel and ducked his head. Songas responded with a proud smile. For the next several sun-ups and sun-downs, Tarias manifested the blade in his head, only taking a break to eat, drink, and relieve himself of waste. Songas urged him to focus entirely and only on the task. As of then, it was Tarias's *only* purpose.

On the seventh day of meditation, Tarias forgot to close his eyes, and soon, the ghostly blade of Adoavi came into reality. Tarias gasped, and Songas's grin of approval made an appearance.

"I told you, Tarias."

Tarias examined the blade. He looked at every edge, every little indentation and marking, trying to burn its image into his head. Before the blade existed, he had only felt the weight in its handle; but with the blade fully evinced, he felt its weight stray closer to its base. After only a moment of intense peering, the blade began to dissolve into the air like sugar in water.

"It is a victory, but not by much. I only have about seven more days."

"Then use those seven days with diligence."

Tarias gritted his teeth and went back to his meditation. However, instead of routinely manifesting in his thoughts, he brought out the blade in front of him, further training his mind. After two days had passed, he could hold the blade for an indefinite time, dependent on his own free choice. Songas held his hand out to Tarias and waved it at him. Tarias assumed he wanted the sword, so he went to give the handle over, but once the blade fell into Songas's hands, the blade dissipated once more.

"Do it again, but do not let the blade disappear. Focus," said the Red Esku, returning the handle to Tarias.

Another two days had passed, and the blade could be maintained after being handed over to the Red Esku, but it could not last for any longer than a moment. Tarias grunted with anger at his inability. Songas placed his hand on Tarias's shoulder. Tarias shook the hand off, for it seemed to feel more like pity than reassurance.

"Remember, I told you the blade does not matter. You have succeeded."

"What do you mean? I cannot keep the blade. How is that a success?"

"You can keep the blade for a moment, and a moment is all you need."

Songas looked at the ladder. He walked right to its base. The trapdoor was closed, so no light could peer through. Songas shifted his eyes over to Tarias.

"You are now able to imagine what does not exist and bring it about, and you are able to do so without touching it," said the Red Esku, dissolving into black particles.

A large thump was heard from the tunnel that led down to the cellar, and dust came floating down from it. In a state of panic, Tarias rushed up the ladder to the trapdoor. He tried to open it, but it would not budge. He was trapped. The Red Esku had trapped him down in the cellar. He could not leave. *He could not leave.* What was he supposed to do? He could not open the trapdoor. He had to stop Adoneir. He had to stop the black-masked elf, but he could not leave.

Tarias closed his eyes and sighed. Once he climbed back down to the cellar floor, he breathed in through his nose and out through his mouth, calming his restless lungs. He closed his eyes and thought of being free. He thought of being outside of the tower and back onto the streets of the Red Aucs. He imagined himself walking the streets, but he opened his eyes and still saw himself inside the cellar. He shook his head in frustration, but then his eyes focused on a fixed point in front of him. It was in front of one of the wardrobes Songas had kept in the cellar. He imagined he was standing in front of it.

Briefly, Tarias felt like he was dissolving, and that every fiber of his being was being stretched and torn apart from each other. Unfortunately, he found that he did not move even a hair away. It took him a while for him to replicate the same feeling. He could not tell exactly how long it took without the aid of outdoor light, but he reckoned it led into the night. The day after, he seemed to be able to replicate the same feeling with more regularity, but he gave up once his body felt drained of any energy to continue.

He opened his eyes, feeling rested. He was unsure how long he had been asleep, but he must have slept well into the next day. He attempted to displace himself almost instinctually after he rose, and this time, his right arm fully disappeared. He failed, but he *almost* succeeded. The small increment of success propelled him to try again and again. He realized, following his exhaustion the day before, that he needed longer periods of rest before attempting displacement, so he gave himself ten counts of sixty in his head until he made another attempt. Gradually, after over several dozen attempts, he stood next to the wardrobe without moving a single muscle. Black dust emanated away from his body, and he smiled.

He walked straight under the ladder and looked up. This time, he did not feel anxiety at the sight of it. Instead, he held determination in his heart. He blinked and found his bare feet resting on top of the cobbled Red Aucs road. Songas sat down on a crate in front of him.

"You did it. You have learned displacement. Good work, Tarias. I guess you can somewhat call yourself a soul seeker now."

Tarias looked at his hands.

"I have learned. It is a strange feeling, but I have learned how."

"Adoneir is much better at it than you are. He has been doing it for years—he knows his limits, you do not. You are to use what you have just learned as a last resort. Do not even think of it as a tool in combat. You will tire yourself and find your neck slit if you do."

Tarias nodded. "Aye, I won't. Thank you."

Songas walked next to Tarias and placed his hand on his shoulder. They were once more in the never-ending field of black mist. Songas held a sword in his hand. Tarias looked down, and he too held a sword. The Red Esku lifted his sword.

"Are we to fight?"

"Yes, but you are to show me how you would use your newfound ability in combat."

Tarias lifted his sword. Tarias felt cold metal go through his intestines. He fell to his knees behind the Red Esku. He collapsed, and soon he lost the strength to keep his eyes open. He opened his eyes. Songas had a sword in hand, and so did Tarias.

"I understand now."

"I am glad you do."

Tarias raised his sword and marched forward. He engaged Songas, and soon their blades clashed against each other. Clangs and sliding metal filled what had been a void of sound. Tarias's body began to disappear, but Songas grabbed him. He *rejected* his displacement and slashed his throat.

Tarias opened his eyes. The Red Esku had a sword in hand, and so did he. He pursued the Esku again while keeping him a blade's length away. He circled him as he sent slashes and thrusts. Songas returned with a proper response, keeping Tarias's blade away. Tarias raised his sword and prepared to slash *down*, and Songas readied his guard to defend. He displaced himself but a few feet below into a kneel, and he thrust the tip of his blade forward. Songas's eyes went wide and his grin stretched ear-to-ear. He displaced himself but half a leg outside of Tarias's sword arm and slashed it, forcing him to drop his blade. The Esku stabbed his blade through Tarias's heart.

Tarias opened his eyes.

"You are a brutal fighter, Songas."

The Esku shrugged.

"I do not enjoy fighting, so I must end the battle quickly. If brutality ends it quickly, then I shall be brutal."

Tarias grinned.

"That is another aspect where we are different, Songas. I *love* to fight."

Tarias readied his sword.

"You do, huh?"

Songas came forward with his blade. Tarias could not say how many duels he had fought or how many deaths he had experienced, but for the remainder of that day, he *fought*.

CHAPTER 16

The streets of Aigerua were a colorful display of blues, yellows, blacks, reds, and greens, with specks of brown scattered in clumps. Tarias could not think of a word to describe what they looked like, but he did smirk at the sight. The Greens never came close to the Yellows and rarely ever fraternized with the Reds. The Blacks seemed to be even more repulsed by the others, so they kept to one large group. The Blues were spread out, but they seemed to hover around the Greens. The Browns kept to themselves as well, for most of them looked a bit shy; however, now and then, a spunky or confident Brown would leave their clump to fraternize with those of another cloth.

Tarias's choice of cloth was Blue. He walked to a bathhouse in the Blue Aucs, on the other side of Aigerua, to change from his gray cloth. Before changing his garments, he made sure to bathe and scrub thoroughly to leave no dirt or stench clinging to him. It seemed many of the other Terukians had the same idea, and there was a bit of a wait before he could acquire a cramped corner in one of the baths. He did not scrub in a hurry. His eyes slowly allowed him to drift asleep.

The bathhouse's steam morphed into black mist, and Tarias was now again dressed. He could not stop his thoughts from circling around the task. It was *his* task. He had never had a task that he had ordered *himself* to do—but it was not like this fact mattered. He had to do his task, and he would succeed. He *had* to succeed.

His 'nap' was truly just meditation. Tarias let his mind drift off into the zephyr that his head now was. His worries were not fully expelled, but their anger had declined into a resting state capable of being steered. Worry had almost killed him last time he was on a task, so worry Tarias would not. He would still plan, for it would be suicide to not plan the execution of a royal. He shuddered at the thought, but he laughed at his hypocrisy. He already killed a royal. What bother could it be if he ended another? Maybe he could end the killing, the insurgency, with the death of Adoneir.

Tarias wondered why Adoneir had ordered the assassination of his cousin. Everything Tarias was taught had led him to value the idea of 'the family'. He did not have a family, so maybe he just could not fathom the intricacies of one; he only had the abstract idea of a family in his head. Yet even though he lacked the experience of family, it still felt strange to him for someone to have their kin murdered. Adoneir must have truly been sick in the mind to stoop to such a depth.

The bathhouse faded back into his view. The density of occupants during festivals annoyed Tarias, but it was nothing he could avoid. He sat and dealt with the hot air that filled the room. He could not tell if the heat was due to the steam itself or to the hot breath of others, but he tried to tell himself it was the steam. A third of the Terukians treated the bath as a place to relax, another third as a place to simply bathe, and the last third as a place to socialize. Tarias treated it as the first two; but unfortunately, whenever so many people visited the bath, the elves who treated the bath as a social gathering tended to drown out the thoughts of the others. Tarias, tired of listening to gossip, stood up, dried himself, and wrapped his body in a blue jant.

He left the bathhouse and gazed out at the roads. There was a smattering of with elves in blue, as Tarias had expected. The Blues wished for more; if one were to look down the road toward the Green Aucs, they would see scattered puddles of Blues turning into clumpy ponds, and finally, at the furthest edge of the Green Aucs, a vast sea of Blues wishing to enter into conversation with the Greens. Tarias ventured forward to reach that sea of Blue. The closer he made it to the Green Aucs, the more he saw of the different colors. He was now in the sea of Blue, which turned into an estuary attempting to mix itself into the Greens and Blacks. Some Greens graciously accepted them, but the Blacks rejected the Blues with a fierce and visible disgust shown by their pompous physiognomy. Tarias kept away from the elves who came from the Black Aucs, for too much trouble would be brought about from them.

After venturing deeper, folk music filled the air with melodies of twangy strings, tooting wind sticks, and gonging percussion instruments. Monks wrapped in gold silks with the vizards of old Emperors guarded a gold and green palanquin that sat in the front of the gates of the Palace of Aigerua. He could see shadowed figure kneeling behind the curtains of the litter. Tarias assumed that this figure was the Koroark, because his brother stood in front of the litter, dressed in a ceremonial gold-and-green patterned jant.

Every year, the brother of the Koroark spoke for him; and after his speech, the palanquin would be lifted and paraded around all the Aucs. All Tarias could do at this moment was wait. Adoneir must have been hidden and cozy in one of the countless buildings that surrounded the Palace while he listened to thoughts, so all Tarias thought of was the Koroark. He made himself *obsess* over the Koroark, for he did not wish to arouse the curiosity of the elf in the broken black mask.

Nakneir's speech was nothing spectacular. The old elf just spoke of the histories of the Terukians with their founding of Aigerua and led a prayer. Everyone knelt. Even the foreigners in the brown robes who stumbled with confusion joined in on the prayer. Tarias focused entirely on the prayer, repeating the lines in his head and waiting until its end. Nakneir finished his prayer, and soon the monks lifted the palanquin. Everyone stood, and they followed the palanquin's route. It went straight for the Blue Aucs, down the same road Tarias had just come from, and once it entered, the palanquin hovered just within the Blue Aucs's border. The Black Aucs Terukians refused to enter the Blue, and even further, when the palanquin had reached the Yellow, they were already waiting in the Red. It seemed the Blacks hated the Sealandesq more than the foreigners. Tarias assumed, within the minds of the Blacks, the difference was that at least there were *some* Midlandesq elves in the Red. The palanquin moved faster in the Blue and Yellow compared to the Green or Red, and as expected, it moved directly toward the Black. Tarias halted. It would be unsafe for him to cross into the Black Aucs with a Blue jant, and it seemed everyone with a Blue or Yellow jant had the same idea.

Tarias's head spun around in search of a stand selling clothes. It would bring him far too much trouble to steal the garb of another, for he had no doubt Adoneir would catch on to the struggle. All the stands sold red. He cursed under his breath, and his eyes aimed at a stand in the Black. It sold black jants, and its owner packed the cloth into a crate and pulled it into his home. Of course, it was around midday, and every elf who wished to attend would have bought a jant by now. The elf left his home and joined the others in the Black.

Tarias found himself standing in the alley next to the house, mist floating away from him. He ran down the alley, but the back of the home connected to the house behind it. With no door in sight, he looked up and saw a window. The crowd was coming, so with haste, he leaped up and pulled himself through the window. He was in a bedroom, devoid of people, that was adorned with green drapes, green blankets, and green rugs. The Blacks sought to emulate the Greens in what seemed to be every manner, whether outside the home or within. He left the bedroom and entered the family room. The crate had been placed by the front entrance, and Tarias hurried for it. He opened it and grabbed a black jant and shawl. They had left their fireplace lit, and Tarias used it to dispose of his blue jant. Now dressed in safer attire, he left the home. The palanquin spent plenty of time in the Black Aucs. Tarias kept his head down the entire time, while he used his peripheral vision to search for Adoneir. Naturally, being a Sealandesq elf, his heart beat slightly faster than usual.

Tarias was in the middle of the crowd of Black Aucs elves. Everyone stopped in their tracks, and for a moment, Tarias thought they were waiting for the palanquin to continue moving. Each person's face stood *frozen* in some expression. Tarias spun around, and some individuals kept their feet hovering with their weight forward. He spun once again to face the palanquin, but blocking its view was an elf in a green jant and black lamellar, grimacing at him with only one visible lip that curled down behind his broken black mask.

"How did you find me? I thought not of you."

"You think like a slave, and your heart pounds like a fearful bitch."

Tarias kept his expression stoic and unflinching.

"Adoneir, you could have stabbed me in my back at any time. Why did you not?"

"You have something I hold a bit of sentiment for. Where is it?"

"I do not hold it, nor will I tell you of it."

Adoneir walked forward with tiny steps. He took his time. He moved with no rush, and his grimacing lip went flat. His hand twitched, and Tarias tried to reach his mind to see what had led it to. The elf's mind was as chaotic as Tarias's, and this revelation led him to stumble back with confusion.

"Neat trick. I have been poking into your head for years. It is amusing that you think you can peek into mine," Adoneir said. "I am giving you the chance to die with some dignity. Kneel and offer your head."

"I will not."

Adoneir drew a blade from his side.

"After today, you shall be headless. I am offering you one last chance to offer your head, yourself, and recommit yourself to the oath you have sworn to me."

"I never swore myself to you. I swore myself to the Koroark."

"My word is the Koroark's own. I order you with the true words of the Emperor. Do know that your life has ended by nothing other than your own treachery."

Tarias bore no sword in his hands and had no sword on his waist. He looked around him to see that all the others stood unarmed as well. However, the shrouded monks carried clubs, and soon, Tarias held one of those clubs in one of his own hands. He now stood at the palanquin; all the Terukians were still frozen, but he felt a hand at his shoulder. He now stood in the vast cobbled square of the Blue Aucs. Tarias pushed Adoneir away. The masked elf stumbled to regain his footing, and Tarias stepped his feet in a fighting stance. The masked elf readied his blade with a grin.

"You didn't have to push me away with such a petty touch. I was going to allow you to get into a stance so that we might have a proper duel. Nonetheless, ready your mind for death."

CHAPTER 17

Adoneir made the first advance forward. He marched his feet slowly, and after reaching a certain distance from Tarias, started to circle his prey. Tarias moved his feet as well. He did not wish to stand still and let the stress of battle cling his feet to the ground. Adoneir had a sword that looked to have a heavy blade, good for cutting, and Tarias's club had a large end that held the majority of the weight. Tarias would have to clobber through Adoneir, and Adoneir would have to cut him down. It was a proper tool for each: clobbering for the armored combatant, and cutting for the elf who only wore a thin cloth robe. Tarias slammed his club up towards Adoneir's hand, but the masked elf simply lifted his guard, and they continued their circling. It was *hard* for him to strike his superior.

"*Fuck.*"

He felt a sharp pain in his knee, and he fell down to a kneel.

"You are a sad little—"

He felt another sharp pain, but this time the pain came from his rib.

"—pathetic, sniveling servant."

Another kick came for him, but it went straight through him. Adoneir fell flat on his backside. Tarias grabbed the club and slammed it down. It hit the elf's lamellar armor, and Adoneir gasped with surprise. Tarias continued to slam while his head was overtaken by an opportunistic frenzy. He did not think of where to slam his club. He was surprised by what happened. What *had* happened? Tarias slowed down, but not to think. A fight was not the time to dwell on current happenings. It was the time to react.

So Adoneir reacted. While Tarias was thinking about not thinking, Adoneir kicked Tarias's stomach. While Tarias was trapped in his thoughts, Adoneir stood up and regained his stance. Tarias's obsession with his own head sent him into an angered frenzy. He stood up. The two again stood at a distance where their weapons could not reach one another, and they began to circle each other *again*.

"Look at you! You are granted a graceful mound of opportunity, and you *throw it away* because you cannot stop your panicked, *pathetic* mind from thinking. This is why you have never and *will* never amount to anything! You think so *damn* much, it even annoys me when I am trying to kill you!"

Tarias readied his club. His eyes were downcast, and his vision contained Adoneir in a tunnel.

"Then think I shall not."

A grin peeked from behind Adoneir's mask. Tarias quickly marched forward to close the distance between the two. Now, with about a leg's distance between the two, Tarias sent a volley of swings. He made the bludgeon look as if it were a feather thrashing in the wind while he spun it. Adoneir leaned to the side, then his other side, up, and then down to evade the swings. One hit him in his side, and he folded without poise. While clutching his side, he swung forward. Maybe he hoped to keep Tarias away, but Tarias did not think of his intentions. Despite suffering a cut to his arm, he trudged forward. He continued to assault Adoneir with crushing blows which put the Green Esku into a stumble.

While Adoneir struggled to stand, Tarias clinched Adoneir's body and sword hand from the front. He snaked around behind him, still clinching down his sword hand, and lifted him while kicking out his knee, forcing him to drop his sword and post both of his hands out in front of him. Tarias readied his hand high while aiming its descent at the crown of Adoneir's head, but the Green Esku sat out, sending the bludgeon into the ground. He tried to wrestle Tarias to the ground, but they found themselves stuck, tying their arms around each other's. They both fought to stand up, and soon the fight devolved into a push and pull of legs and pummeling of arms.

Tarias dragged Adoneir's arm to the side and swam that same arm around the Green Esku's neck while he moved to his back. He *squeezed*. Adoneir remained calm while he scurried his hands about, looking for an escape; but every time he attempted something, Tarias shot it down with a counter.

Tarias grinned while he squeezed. He was almost there. He would finally bring justice to Elreina and clear his conscience.

Then Adoneir disappeared. Tarias felt a hand cupping the front of his neck. He was set into a free fall, flailing to the ground. It felt like someone had kicked his legs out from under him, and he stared at the sky with confusion. Adoneir fell to his knees while his fist slammed like a hammer into Tarias's face. Tarias felt his airpipe compress. The masked elf squeezed the soul seeker's neck and slammed his head into the ground.

Tarias could not breathe. Of course he could not breathe, he was being choked. He was cold and wet. His eyes stung, and air bubbles seemed to cover the entirety of his view. His arms fearfully reached around in an effort to grab anything he could. Adoneir continued to slam Tarias's head into the ground, but it felt like there was more resistance. It felt like something was in the way of his head being slammed, despite his skull still being sent backward. Was he underwater? He felt a burning sensation in his lungs, and his agitated heart shook his body with primal panic.

Tarias felt his body being pulled up. Water dripped down from his hair while a dead look lingered on his face. Adoneir had a grin on his face. It looked like he enjoyed suffocating Tarias. Tarias could not produce the effort to react. He felt robbed of energy.

"You were so close, Tarias. You had potential, but your pathetic mind could only produce failure and disappointment from all those around you. If you would have only aligned yourself with me, you could have been afforded a degree of pity; but you wish to aid the *false* Koroark instead. Now, I take your head."

Adoneir pulled another blade from his side. Tarias stared towards the sky, and his head was forced down into a bow. The cold edge of the blade rested on his neck, and Adoneir lifted it up.

"Interesting. So that is who you accept to be the true Koroark," said a familiar voice.

Tarias's looked up. Adoneir looked over as well, and they were both met with the sight of Songas. He sat with a lackadaisical swagger while his legs were crossed on the rim of the fountain. This time, he did not have the grin he always wore. His angered face was almost as red as the jant that covered him. Adoneir stood up straight with the blade loosely wrapped in his fingers. His grin straightened and pursed to hold back what looked to be an annoyance that filled him.

"There is no use going around it now, I suppose. Are you happy now that your suspicions were confirmed? Does it truly please you now that I have nothing left to lose?"

"I always wondered why you hid your thoughts and face so fervently. You did not wish for anything to leak out. You are the most secretive of the Eskus. Adoneir, why did you betray your family?"

Adoneir's grip tightened. "The mound was never my uncle's to have. He did not *deserve* it, and neither did Elreina deserve to be its inheritor."

Songas stepped into the fountain waters and walked forward without urgency. Adoneir raised his blade high and looked at Tarias's nape. Without hesitation, Songas produced a golden handle from his jant. Tarias's eyes widened, and Adoneir whipped his hand forward to point at the Red Esku.

"So you carry it? Hand over that blade."

"This handle is all that remains of it, no?"

Adoneir looked down at Songas. The Red Esku juggled the hilt and let it fall into his grasp. He held the handle with a firm hand, and he stuck his arm out toward one of the three grated fire pits that surrounded the base of the statue. Clear particulates were pulled from the air, and soon the blade was an arrow pointing at the fire pit. Songas turned his head and walked towards the pit.

Adoneir ran for the Red Esku. Songas turned so that the blade would meet Adoneir's arrival. The masked elf displaced and appeared in front of Songas while he reached for his sword arm. Songas, reacting quicker than a cat, yanked his arm up. Then he slashed his elbow down like it was a cutting sword, causing the Green Esku's mask to crack more from where it had originally been broken.

Tarias crawled to them with his hands dipping in and out of the fountain water. He made it to the rim, and he used what strength he had recovered to pull himself up. Now standing, he watched the two Eskus engage. He expected them to be quick, but they only inched while they circled each other. They both looked to be cautious, like they did not know what would happen. He could sense some respect between the two; or, at least, they respected each other's ability in combat. He squinted his eyes. The entirety of his mind focused on them, for the outcome of this duel, at this moment, was the only thing that mattered to Tarias.

Songas stepped forward, his sword tip facing down. Adoneir, in response, shifted his sword hand not high nor low, but pointed it forward. Adoneir attacked, and Songas swiped upwards with the blade. The masked elf also had quick reflexes. He parried the attack and stabbed forward with his sword.

"Songas!" cried Tarias.

The Red Esku collapsed with a grin.

Tarias's eyes opened. Songas still stood where he had been standing before, and he did not step forward. Adoneir's face darted between Tarias and Songas. Tarias could feel his anger manifest into heat. Adoneir turned to Songas and sent a flurry of passionate attacks at the Red Esku. Tarias smiled, for Songas truly was an aggravating fellow. Songas moved as if he knew what Adoneir would do next, and with every swing of Adoneir's sword, the Red Esku's sly grin grew wider. He paced backward toward the fire pit. He aimed his steps for the center of it, where the grate was open for the disposal of sacrificial offerings. Tarias's mind was a tornado of worry, and he forced himself to stumble towards the two.

The Red Esku continued to pace backward. Adoneir still sent a flurry of attacks, but the more he attempted to strike the Red Esku, the more manic he became. He gritted his teeth, and he choked the handle of his blade. Once they crossed over the grate, Adoneir sent another strike. Songas parried it, and upon impact, Adoneir's blade rattled in his hands and slipped from his grasp down into the yellow flames of the fire pit. Songas punched the Esku in the mask, allowing what had been cracked to fall down into the fire pit below. Adoneir stumbled, and the Red Esku sent his ghostly blade up to sever the black masked elf's arm clean off from the shoulder. Adoneir gasped in horror at the sight of losing his sword arm. Tarias, now behind Adoneir, sent his foot into the side of the Green Esku's knee, sending him down the fire pit into the yellow flames below.

Songas and Tarias stared down into the depths of the flames, watching the fire slowly cook the body of the masked elf. Songas grasped Tarias's shoulder and displaced the two back outside the tower in the Red Aucs.

"I thought you could not aid me," Tarias said.

"I did not speak the full truth. I had to see Adoneir's treachery for myself."

CHAPTER 18

The two walked into the tower and climbed down once more into its depths. After his feet tapped the chamber's floor, Songas walked to one of the shelves and put down the handle of Adoavi. Tarias walked up to it.

"I do not understand. I thought you died, yet here you stand living."

"I have experienced your thoughts. You saw my death, and I saw the same. I changed my actions so that I would not die."

Tarias brushed his finger along the gold handle.

"What did it matter if you took this blade to the fire pits? What would it have changed, and why did Adoneir care?"

"Particular objects, such as Adoavi's blade, cannot only be brought back from the past, but their history can be experienced the same way I experience another's thoughts. That blade is similar to a book, but it is worth more than that. You cannot copy it. You cannot simply order a scribe to copy its words and form a new book. It is one of a kind, and if Adoneir's loss of it leads to its destruction, then he is surely up for a harsh reprimand."

"There has to be something more to it. You interrupted his train of thought. He was going to take my head, but you stopped him."

"There *is* more to it, but you will not understand until you experience it."

Tarias reached for the handle. He held its gleaming gold handle in his hands.

"How do I experience it?"

"I will not tell you. You are not in a proper frame of mind *to* experience it. Not only that, we have more important matters to deal with."

Frustrated, Tarias gripped the handle tighter; but he halted his anger and placed the handle back where Songas had left it. Songas knelt to meditate, and Tarias joined him.

"What did you learn?" Tarias asked.

"The mind is truly a fickle thing, and those who are experienced in our line of work know this well; yet people are people, and none of us are perfect. Those who last are those who have survived all of their past mistakes, and they tend to be the ones who make the least amount of them. Adoneir has always been entitled. He was gifted, but his talent made him reckless, especially when it came to combat. Whenever he was near victory, he would always allow a glimpse into his mind, and when he exclaimed that the Koroark was false, he thought of who he believed to be the *true* Koroark."

"And who would that be?"

"Nakneir."

"Do you believe Nakneir betrayed his brother?"

"If not before, he surely will now with the death of his son. When it comes to the history between the Koroark and his brother, there can be enough reason to say that Nakneir covets the mound. With the death of Elreina, the line of succession goes to Nakneir. Furthermore, because Adoneir is the firstborn of Nakneir, he would be second-in-line."

Tarias stared at the floor of the cellar.

"I killed Elreina. I pushed Adoneir to his demise. If I were to be the elf who killed Nakneir, then I would have killed the Koroark's whole family. I do not see a future for myself."

"We must investigate Nakneir. There is no going around it. I must safeguard the Emperor, even if it is from his own brother."

"And what must I do?"

"I do not know yet. Give me time to deliberate on our next move. I will go back to the Palace in search of any evidence of treachery. If you wish to help, use your gift to see what might happen."

"I do not know how."

"You do know, for you already used it. Do it again."

Songas displaced, leaving Tarias alone in the hole. He sat wondering what to do, and because he had come to no conclusion, he displaced himself. The Cloth Festival still continued, and Tarias reckoned there was little time before they reached the Palace. This was perfect for Tarias, for the crowds would be away from him. He had time to return to Adoneir's body and look at it.

Displacement took quite a toll on one's body, and Tarias was experiencing that toll. The grinding feeling of displacement was one thing, but actually initiating it was another. He was *drained.* It was like his past displacements earlier that day had built up. He laughed at himself, for now he would have to walk a good while until he could displace himself the rest of the way. He did not take his time; however, it was hard to trudge forward when the warm sun felt cozy when he closed his eyes to blink.

What would have been an instantaneous travel turned into a leg-aching journey. It came as a shock, as Tarias knew he was conditioned for running this distance, yet his mind beckoned him to sit down once he reached about halfway. He did sit down. His tired eyes wandered around the streets, looking at the hitched azkozals and the running waters. The trees that lined these roads grew or were pruned to look like covered longships, the branches which extended from the trunk growing out in the shape of a hull, and their green leaves covering their tops, protecting them from the sky. He sat under one of these trees, and he welcomed its shade. He had never noticed their shape. He always found himself looking down instead of up, so he took the moment to appreciate their beauty.

After he felt his strength return to him, Tarias stood, and he roamed down the road toward the Statue of Ee'nak. There were several people there. The Koroark must have returned to the Palace by now. With caution, he wandered to the grate where Adoneir had fallen; but when he stared down through the grate, he discovered that the elf's body was gone.

Had he been incinerated already? Could Tarias not see his body through the flames? Whatever it was, the masked elf was done. He was dead. Tarias focused down into the pit. His gaze delved into the fire. His vision was surrounded by turbulent yellow flames, and his head felt warm. His skin cooked from the heat. It grew so intense that beads of sweat began to form in an effort to cool Tarias's skin.

He was transported back to the morning after the day Elreina's lover had killed himself. He sat low, and he saw the guards pull the elf in the brown robes out of the water of the fountain. He felt a breeze *in* his neck. He looked down to see his wooly body fall into the flames of the grate below. He felt the searing hot pain. He felt his flesh being cooked off of his body. He felt death.

His eyes shot open. He stood above the grate, still remembering the feeling of his flesh being burnt. His irritation almost burned as hot as the heat he had experienced. He looked once more back into the grate and *focused*.

He found himself looking at a mirror and saw a face he had not ever seen before. He walked around his room, and there was a stuffed leather bag on top of the bed. The garments inside were green. He threw the bag over his shoulder and made his way out the door.

Tarias recognized the hallway immediately. He stood in the Palace of Aigerua. Immediately after exiting the room, he noticed a young elfe in a green dress pacing back and forth clutching her head with distress. To her side, an elf dressed in red stood grinning whenever he was out of sight from the young elfe's gaze.

"Elreina, what is wrong?"

"I cannot find my hair ribbon, Adoneir, have you seen it? I have been looking everywhere, and I cannot find it."

Tarias's gaze shifted to Songas, and Songas smirked.

"Songas, a moment."

His hand waved for the young elf to follow him. Adoneir grabbed Songas's wrist and pulled him down the hall. They found themselves in a spot where it was much quieter, a place where Elreina's worries were a little less loud.

"Quit tormenting her, Songas. Grow up a little. You pride yourself in being kind, yet you always pull stupid tricks like this."

"It is harmless, Adoneir. It is just a ribbon. I planned on giving it back anyway."

"When? When she was just about to leave? It is very rude to do such a thing to someone. You know Elreina is very picky about her appearance when we travel."

Tarias looked Songas up and down. He tried to read the elf's thoughts to find where he had placed the ribbon, but he could not. All he saw were his own thoughts and the worried thoughts of Elreina.

"Songas… to read your thoughts is to read the world's. Where did you place the ribbon?"

Songas did not speak.

"Songas… Where?"

"In truth, Adoneir, I lost it…"

"You just said you were going to give it back."

"That was a lie, Adoneir. I was going to replace it."

Tarias shook his head with disappointment. He stormed off down the hall. In truth, this was not his problem, so he would let Songas deal with his wrongdoing alone. He strolled his way to the mound. His uncle was not present, but his father was. His father stood, staring at, *longing for*, the mound.

"Greetings, son," said Nakneir.

"Hello, Father. What are you doing?"

"Come, son. Stand next to me."

Tarias did not disobey. He walked to Nakneir's side. He noticed something strange about his skin. It had a slight glow and faint geometric patterns that could barely be seen. Tarias stared a bit too long, and he caught a leer from Nakneir.

"So, you have touched the mound?" Tarias asked.

Nakneir looked down.

"Father, you know the punishment for that is death."

"And that is why you shall say nothing."

Tarias looked down. His glare was empty, for he glared at nothing but his own worries.

"I could hide it from the everyman, but from uncle? I would soon be on the chopping block next to you. I cannot see a future where I can hide it from him."

Nakneir reached for a mask that hung at his side. It was black, and it looked like a creature he had heard of in stories his mentors had told him. Another elf used to wear that mask, and that elf was always at the side of the Koroark.

"Adoneir, I did not want you to take on the duty of a soul seeker, but now I *need* you to take on the duty of an Esku."

"What?"

"The Esku of the Green Aucs is no more, and now with the position's vacancy, we need a new one. There is no better option than you."

"Yogis? How did Yogis die?"

Nakneir glared at his son, and Tarias immediately knew what he wished to say.

"Take the mask, son. You are now the Green Esku."

Nakneir handed him the mask. The feeling of it drained the strength from him, and his thoughts slowly became less and less lucid. He placed the mask onto his face.

Tarias awoke. He was now on his knees, aching with the pressure of the metal grate below him. That was it? He needed more information. He leaned forward on the grate and stared down into the white-yellow flames. Tarias gripped the grate so firmly that he thought he would crush it between his fingers.

He saw his hands cuffed. He was alone. A chain extended from the cuffs, and an elf wearing green dragged him to the Palace of Aigerua. He was past the gate at this moment, and his tired body was pulled to the steps. His heart pounded.

Every time Tarias's feet stuck to the ground for a little too long, the guards would yank him forward. He was not allowed a moment of rest.

The mound of the Koroark was before him now, and an older elf sat cross-legged on top. Tarias, now on the grass in front of the mound, was forced to his knees by the guard. As soon as his knees hit the ground under him, his head was forced to face downcast. Tarias deserved his fate. He deserved to die at the hands of the Koroark. He felt his body heat up while beads of sweat fell from his head. His heart pounded, and after feeling a sharp pain at the back of his neck, his head fell to the grass-covered ground.

CHAPTER 19

Tarias felt a big lump on his forehead. He noticed it was raw, and it stung like it had just been pressed against a hot brand. He was being pulled up by individuals dressed in brown robes. He laughed to himself, for it would have had to be a foreigner to help him. A Midlandesq elf would think it too strange to help a Sealandesq elf in black, and a Sealandesq elf would have too much malice or fear for a Black Aucs elf. But a foreigner? They would not know the slightest difference. To a foreigner, all elves were the same. They were like mankind but with sharper jaws and pointier ears. If mankind was a raw boulder, Terukians were carved arrowheads.

There was not just a man who wore brown helping Tarias up, but two green okrs and a Sombraski elf as well. The Sombraski were treated more poorly than even the Sealandesq elves. Tarias was shocked to see one in the capital.

"A Sombraski elf? What brings your kind here?"

"What brought you to wear the clothes of your betters? At least I wear appropriate attire," snarked the elf.

The Sombraski was right. Tarias still wore the colors of a Black Aucs elf. How clumsy of him. He could already hear Songas in his ear, muttering *not a true soul seeker*.

The group left Tarias by himself, and Tarias sat wondering who he was. He had killed his superior. He killed his *purpose*. It was a strange thing. He was nothing. After a moment, Tarias ran toward the posse of foreigners, his desperate feet leaping himself forward.

"I give you all thanks for your help! May I ask who you are?"

This time, the man turned his head around to face Tarias.

"We are the Cheery Folk! We are a band of travelers who

have met each other throughout the most austere moments of our lives. I am Inel, the two green twins are Retsiuks and Ieutsnakis, and the Sombraski elf is Onigos."

They did not look to carry weapons, but the way they carried themselves insinuated that weaponry was not foreign to them.

"How did you meet?"

Each individual in the group smirked. They all looked to Retsiuks and Ieutsnakis. The two were a little less brutish-looking for okrs, but they still had the poking underbite of one. Their smirks were frightening to look at. It was like Tarias was being stared down by a predator. The one closest to Inel stepped forward. He had a chipped tooth and a scar on his cheek, both on the right of his face.

"We met each other on a slaver's podium in the Sealands."

The okr's voice was cheery. Irony led Tarias to grin.

"You dare laugh at Retsiuks saying he was a slave?"

"No! Of course not. I found—"

Inel held his hand palm up. "We know why you laughed. It is quite hilarious to hear such a happy okr. They are portrayed to be wild things that roam and pillage, but Retsiuks and Ieutsnakis here are civilized."

Ieutsnakis shook his head.

"So, why is a man in Aigerua?"

"Well, because I bought these three and freed them."

Tarias shook his head. "That does not make sense. Why would you free them for no reason? What benefit does it bring you?"

"What do you mean, no reason? Why must there be a reason?"

"Without reason, we would wander aimlessly."

"What was their reason to be enslaved?"

"I do not know their history."

Inel pointed to the two okrs. "They were born in a greenfolk village that was raided by one of the city-states in the Sealands. They were taken when they were children, and that is why they are so soft-spoken. They were raised with the manners of the Sealands. They were raised to obey despite their nature."

Inel pointed to Onigos. "He was a young potter, but he is a Sombraski. They plucked him off the streets by the people of the same city-state that slaughtered Rets's and Ieuts's village. He was forced to obey. *Despite* his nature."

"What is in their nature that makes that so?"

"The only thing that separates us from each other. Our *will*. It was never in their will to be a slave. They did not ask for it."

Tarias remembered what Adoneir had said. The phrase *you think like a slave* rang in his head. What made Tarias think like a slave? What was he a slave to?

"This seemed to have struck something in you," said the soft voice of Retsiuks.

Tarias looked off at the crowds with a dim glare. His face carried consternation, and his jaw drooped under the weight of it. He was over-aware of his thoughts, but now, they were less like a frenzied storm and had become slightly calmer. It was immediate, one thought after another, and they hazed the perimeter of Tarias's view. They dulled his ability to hear. Soon, it was like he was standing in the black mists of his mind.

A pat on his shoulder. Inel rested his palm on Tarias. He held him firm, and within his eyes was deep worry. He removed his hand, and Tarias faced him.

"What worries you?"

"I think like a slave," Tarias said. "I have no want other than to serve."

The Cheery Folk grinned. Ieutsnakis came forward with crossed arms and a smile. His palm stuck out and he held it open to the sky.

"No one thinks like a slave. People can only *be* enslaved, but your will to serve is just that: your will. It may not be what you ultimately want—maybe that changes—but as of right now, you wish to serve. Coincidentally, we of the Cheery Folk all hold that same want. What is worthy of your service?"

"What is worthy of yours?" asked Tarias.

"Liberation," replied Onigos.

"Justice," stated Retsiuks.

"To protect my family," followed Ieutsnakis, putting a hand on his brother's shoulder.

Inel looked away. He held a grimace on his face. "To right my wrongs."

Tarias shifted his view to Inel. The man's face was filled with woe. Tarias felt the man's sadness, so he turned his head to hide his curiosity. Tarias stared down in thought. It was simple: he *had* to kill Nakneir. But why? Why must he do anything at all? What pushed him to? What was the reason behind his drive?

"You are lost. The question Ieuts asked must have made your heart race."

"How could you tell?" Tarias asked.

"You wear your worry on your face. We often express our woes when thinking of something that truly troubles us. You do not know your own will."

"I only wish for one thing, and I cannot share what it is."

Inel smiled. "You do not need to share. As of now, that is your purpose."

Onigos had a mean look on his face. It was almost like how some Sealandesq elves glared at Midlandesq elves when they knew they would not be seen. He was resented by the elf, and that elf was the first to wave goodbye. The rest followed. Shockingly, Inel, a *man*, waved goodbye with a smile. It was unlike what Tarias had been taught of foreigners. Perhaps these truly were Cheery Folk.

Tarias looked back to the tower, and he strode there with a better sense of direction than when he had strode to the Statue of Ee'nak. Songas was waiting outside. He had a sour look on his face, and it grew even more sour upon Tarias's arrival.

"What is it, Songas?"

"Nakneir is planning something. I snuck around his personal guard, and he ordered them to prepare items such as explosives."

"When will it happen?"

Songas was calm, but a faint huff of his breath signaled his disappointment.

"I do not know. I know it is soon, but I cannot experience thoughts that do not exist. He has them all on a need-to-know basis. I tried to poke for leaks, but there simply are none."

"Nakneir touched the mound."

"I know. I experienced your thoughts. They are much calmer now. I can delineate which ones are which with far less effort."

"I figured you did. I saw your already upset expression worsen upon my arrival."

"No, that is only because you are now here," retorted Songas with a raised brow and sly grin.

Songas clenched his jaw. Stress seemed to pull on his muscles.

"I have to report this to the Koroark, but Nakneir is always around him. He would surely contest, and once he knows I am working with *you*, there would be no arguing against it."

Tarias stared down. "Nakneir has come into contact with the past Koroarks. He has access to all-powerful knowledge."

Songas shrugged. "Maybe."

"What do you mean? It is the mound of the Koroark. It gives access to the lives of the past Emperors!"

"He was only on it for at most a moment. Imagine attempting to read a book for a moment; it would be a shock that someone would be able to read even a fraction of a page."

"Time matters?"

"Time always matters. You may not be aware of it when you are in such a state, but I have killed people before they could finish their thoughts. Nakneir probably believes he has had some divine revelation that could put him on par with the Koroark if he is acting against him. It is foolishly wrought hubris."

Tarias came closer to the tower. He looked up to it, then his gaze fell to stare at the ground. He opened its doors and looked at the broken ladder.

"Why did you choose to go down and not up? Surely the thoughts of others should be muted from up there as well. What is up there?"

"Nothing is up there, and it is not quiet enough," said Songas walking in behind him.

"You do well around others, Songas. Surely you have learned to control it better."

Songas snickered. "Control? I cannot control it. They are intrusive. Apparently, others have intrusive thoughts as well, but those thoughts are born from their own mind. My intrusive thoughts are born from others. Adoneir was known for his ability to guard his thoughts. He had a gift like mine, like yours, but what separates my gift from yours is that I cannot *control* my thoughts at all. It is like a roaring river where no engineer would even fathom putting up a dam, for it would be ripped to shreds by its violent torrent. I am forbidden to leave Aigerua unless ordered. Ideally, I would be in the middle of nowhere, but that is not possible. I must stay in the Red Aucs, and the only place I may have the solitude of silence is far underneath the ground."

"I assume Nakneir has a gift as well? Adoneir had one, and the Koroark is the most gifted. What is his?"

"I do not know. We are at a disadvantage, surely."

Songas looked down and shifted his robes. A satchel was revealed, and he pulled out a dagger.

"Nothing can be perfectly cleaned. There must be some residue left on this blade, and I believe your gift is simply a far more potent ability to *read*."

"What do you mean?"

"Not only did you see the future—your *death*—you saw the past."

Tarias realized something.

"You loved Elreina," he said. "That was why you said I deserved it. I could tell you truly wanted me dead. What stopped you from doing so? I would not have been able to stop you."

"You felt genuine guilt. My gift would have been fine if I was not cursed with empathy, but honestly, I would not want to see a world where an elf like Nakneir had my gift. It would be a dark world. Nakneir always had the makings of a tyrant."

Tarias reached forward to grab the dagger. He frowned with hesitation. He remembered when he had last used his gift. He saw his death. He feared what he would see now. He feared that he would see their failure.

"Worry not, Tarias. Focus."

CHAPTER 20

The dagger held two edges. It had no quillons, but this did not matter because its curved handle had a ring where a finger would go to prevent the blade from sliding against the user's hand. It was very plain for how strange the design was, compared to the knives Tarias was used to. It must have been made by special request, for it bore no touchmark and was of a design Tarias had never seen carried by anyone in Aigerua.

"I wish I could say those in our line of profession were absent of flaws, but people are people. They have their quirks, and Nakneir's quirk is his insistence on killing everyone with the same knife."

Tarias chuckled. "That is interesting. I suppose my quirk is that I insist on keeping nothing."

"Maybe; or maybe it is all you know. You were groomed to be the way you are."

"Nakneir comes from power, from rulership, and you were taken under their wing. Maybe *you* were groomed to think that way."

"Maybe, Tarias—but honestly, you do know most people carry possessions, don't you? Pretty much everyone owns something. You walk around with only that gray robe, and I have read your thoughts. You would throw that robe away if the act would not draw eyes to you."

Tarias chuckled and waved Songas away as he began to climb down into the chamber. It was just how they left it, but Adoavi's blade was already placed away on the shelf. Tarias looked at it, and then he looked back to Nakneir's dagger.

"Would reading this dagger be the same as reading Adoavi's blade?"

"It would be easier. It still exists. Nonetheless, it is the same."

"He is old. If this blade was what he used to kill all of his foes, then surely it would take a long while to find anything useful."

"Then hurry, Tarias."

Tarias stared down at the blade and squinted his eyes. He tried to forget everything else around him. The nature of the room made it easy to do so, and it was not long until his mind was drifting into memories that were not his own. He experienced death repetitively. He felt the lack of awareness as well as the sudden rush of fear that shot into him once he felt the blade puncture his body. He experienced the memories of people from numerous walks of life: crafts-elves, a painter, soldiers, Nagusi, a few Arks, wives, and *children*. Every so often, these experiences would rip him out of their memories in a cold sweat. He knew the feeling of killing someone, but now he felt the true fear of the victims. At times, he did not even grasp that these were the experiences of another, for he felt them as if they were his own.

He was sad. He felt like the world was crumbling around him. His feet were heavy with his sorrow, and they dragged across the Aigeruan road. The sun was bright, but it still felt gloomy. It was like he was dead, but he could still breathe and experience the world; however, it did not matter to him. He had no opinion of the world. All he wanted was to *leave* the world. He choked a dagger in his hand, but it was not Nakneir's.

Now at the rim of the statue's fountain, he climbed up and in. He felt his brown jant dampen while he sat down in the water. His hand shook while he lifted the blade and pointed it to his forearm. It sliced into his flesh, and a stream of blood flowed from the crook of his elbow to his wrist. He moved the blade to his other hand and hurried to do the same to his other wrist, but the wrist of the arm that held the dagger was grabbed by the hand of another elf. This elf wore a black jant and a black shawl to cover his face from view.

"Allow me to finish you off, you sniveling ordinary."

The elf in black slit the elf's other wrist. His sad eyes looked up with awe. He felt like he was sinking further and further into the fountain, and soon, his vision faded away.

Tarias wept.

"Sometimes, the memories follow you," muttered Songas.

"I do not see the reasoning for killing the merchant. He was already dead."

"Nakneir is an over-glorified savage. Every minor thing is personal to him. I imagine he killed him because he was the father of Elreina's child, and in Nakneir's mind, because the elf was of the commonfolk, he deserved to die."

Tarias entered once more the minds of the dead. He felt hunger. He felt desire. His hands were rotted and his sharp teeth decayed. He was in battle with Nakneir, and soon, dead in his black blood.

A sword dropped to his feet. The coast was rocky, and waves crashed onto them under the shiny summer sun. Tarias wore the metal of a decorated Nagus. He stared down at his slit throat, marking his defeat.

Sand surrounded Tarias, and his hands crashed down onto the dry ground. The heat stole the energy from him. Thirst was the only thing on his mind, but the shining waters of an oasis were nowhere in sight. In fact, the only shiny object was the blade that he thrust into his own heart.

Tarias stared at his punctured chest. Blood stained his green jant, and his black mask fell to the ground, staring up at him. Nakneir grabbed him by the collar and pulled him up. He reached for the blade, but his broken arms ignored the pleas of his brain.

"I have always known you were despicable, Nakneir. You are a stain on Teruk."

Nakneir's fist crashed into Yogis's face. Three teeth flew out onto the ground in a splatter of blood. Nakneir pulled Yogis up by his hair, and Tarias felt them almost rip from their follicles. He felt his mind explode. He could not make sense of anything. It was a whirlwind of incoherence.

Tarias pulled himself back out and rubbed his eyes. Songas had his brow raised with concern. After placing the dagger down, Tarias stood up to lean against a stray crate in the room. His mind was spinning, and he buckled down from resting his hands on the crate rim to his elbows. He felt like whatever he ate earlier was about to bid him goodbye.

"Do you have any water, Songas?"

"I do not keep any down here. Do you want me to fetch you some?"

"No, no," said Tarias, waving his hand. "I will be fine. It is beginning to go away."

"You have had the experiences follow you more than once today. That is a strange occurrence, but with how vividly you see the visions, I suspect it is not coincidental. Take a rest, Tarias."

Tarias nodded. Songas was probably right, for he felt he needed to sit down and collect his thoughts. He fumbled around the room for a piece of parchment. There was no possible way that he could remember these visions as vividly as he had experienced them. He needed to write them down for them to be worth their struggle. Songas walked over to his desk and retrieved parchment, ink, and a writing implement. Tarias jotted the visions down.

"They are strange visions, most of them, and one of them is a suicide. The blade must be old, or at some point lost," said Songas.

The Red Esku handed Tarias a small knife.

"Prick your finger and leave a blood stain on the bottom right corner. Since your experiences are fresh, the memories from your blood would also be fresh."

Tarias pricked his finger and did as Songas had said. Songas grabbed the knife, and he displaced. He returned moments after, but now, he did not have the blade in hand.

"I destroyed it. No one ought to have access to your thoughts."

Tarias did not question Songas's honesty. He had learned thus far that Songas was the most trustworthy person he had ever met. He was taught that he should always question those who sought to be a friend or ally, but Songas had always proved to be genuine. He struggled to believe there was a malevolent bone in his body.

"Why did you do nothing about the merchant and Elreina? Their marriage was unlawful, and you loved her," Tarias said.

Songas grinned. "What makes you ask that?"

"Surely you would have known. The merchant would have felt love for her, and you would have felt his thoughts."

"I did not do anything about it *because* I loved her."

"How does that help?"

"I am a soul seeker. An *Esku*. There is no world where I would have been able to marry a presumptive Koroarka. I was an orphan, and the only reason I was able to be in her presence was by the grace of the Koroark."

"How could the Koroark not hear of it?"

"I am not allowed to say, but I am certain he does not know of it."

Tarias shuddered. "You did not tell him? Why?"

Tarias saw Songas's anger once more. He stumbled back.

"He would have delivered her the same fate you gave her. I wanted to prevent that. She loved that merchant. That memory you have, when she argued with him just before you killed her—they were arguing about their *child*. They were arguing about her not being able to be with him. His name was Uebyel. He wanted her to run away with him. He was a rich merchant who could travel the world, and she was the heir apparent to the Realm of the Elves. She was Teruk's future, so she painfully told him they were done. I felt his pain like it was my own. It was worse than my own feelings of loss for her."

"What is the point in keeping possessions or maintaining relations if we cannot enjoy them?"

Songas kept his head down. "You know how haunting our profession is. These possessions, and my friendships, all remind me that despite all the bad that surrounds us, there is still some good in the world. So, I latch onto them. They are important to me."

Tarias stared at Nakneir's dagger. "I imagine Nakneir would want to have this back. He would come for it."

"Yes, indeed he would. He does not do much killing nowadays, but once he figures out his son is dead, he would want to kill us with that blade."

"You are an Esku, and you dwell in the Red Aucs. Adoneir was the Esku of the Green Aucs. In my visions, Nakneir wore black. Is he the Black Esku?"

"Yes."

"How many soul seekers does he have under him?"

"We never share that information with other Eskus, and we are forbidden from investigating each other. But Nakneir is the oldest of us all, so he would have a few under him. No more than ten, but no less than three, I would assume."

"There are Eskus of the Blue and Yellow Aucs, right? Would they aid us?"

"The Yellow Esku is too preoccupied with matters in the Yellow Aucs. The Blue Esku might. He is a zealous and inquisitive fellow, however, so I do not know how well he would react to infighting amongst the Eskus. I would have to speak with him."

"How many soul seekers are under you?"

"I never sought to recruit others. I never expected an event like this to occur."

"Well, if we are going to fight, we will have to choose a proper location. Somewhere flat and unpopulated. I have noticed my ability requires that I see my target directly, or that I have them in my own hands—and we do not want to have your ability to think restricted by a crowd."

"Good thinking, Tarias. I will seek out the Blue Esku, and you will find our battleground."

CHAPTER 21

Tarias wandered around Aigerua. He soon came to realize that there would be no place or time where the city would be a suitable place to fight. Throughout the day, the streets were flooded with travelers and marketgoers. In the night, there would not be silence for Songas, for the houses were so close together that dreams and nightmares would intrude on the Red Esku's mind. He thought back to when he had lost, to when Songas saved him in the Yellow Aucs's sewer, and he set out to find the field where he had awoken next to Songas. It was not the perfect spot for a battle, but compared to the city, it was far better.

He walked to the edge of the outer Aigeruan walls and displaced himself outside. With the memory of the fatigue that followed from displacing at a large distance, Tarias limited himself to about a dozen yards. He felt dizzy after repetitive displacement, and he stumbled around like a dog with a lame leg. This was a far distance from the tower, *very* far. Tarias laughed to himself while he fell to the ground. He lay flat on his back and stared at the sky with his arms splayed out like a stretched cat. Frequency must have been a limit as well.

He allowed himself a nap. He felt like he could use one. When his vision drifted away into the unconscious, he saw nothing. There were no dreams, nightmares, visions, or even the lucidity of knowing that one was dreaming of nothing. Maybe once he woke up, he immediately forgot that he was dreaming. Thankfully, the rest that the nap delivered to him was refreshing, and he felt like he could have displaced right after standing up.

By now, it was night. The torchlight that filled the streets of Aigerua made the city look like a lantern from his distance.

They would have to lure Nakneir out; but because he was a sentimental elf, Tarias reckoned he would want to kill him himself.

Tarias walked back to the walls and displaced himself inside. He assumed he would walk the rest of the way to the Red Aucs. He returned to the tower. Songas stood there with an elf in blue, and they looked to be deep in discussion. The elf in the blue had his arms crossed with his feet pointing away from Songas. His jaw was clenched, and this sight pumped anxiety throughout Tarias's body. He looked at Tarias and grimaced.

"Songas, I do not understand what could possess you to work with such a despicable waste of flesh." The Blue Esku spat on the ground before Tarias's feet.

Tarias was about to speak in response, but Songas's eyes went wide. Tarias took it as a warning not to talk. The Blue Esku shook his head and grunted. He shot his arm out and violently pointed at Tarias.

"That elf ought to die! He killed the heiress. No matter his utility, he ought to *die*."

Songas shook his head. "You are too zealous for forethought. The Koroark may soon die, and Tarias is the only elf to be able to see the future. He is the only one that can save him from that fate."

"Fuck his gift. He is a criminal, a *heretic*."

"And what gift do you have?" asked Tarias.

Songas shot the elf a fearful side-eye. The Blue Esku uncrossed his arms and raised both of his fists. They trembled with anger.

"What gift? My *hands* are my gift."

Songas placed his hand on the Blue Esku's shoulder. The elf calmed down slightly and lowered his fists.

"Uindok does not tire; or, rather, he does tire, but he does not stop. You can cut him any number of times, and he will not slow down his advance. He is the Fist of Aigerua."

Uindok's look of disapproval did not leave his face. It was obvious he was not fond of Tarias with the way he was so on guard around him. His vigilance was not a symptom of fear, for he did not flinch at Tarias's movements. He stared him down with repugnance. If there was a wall between the two, passersby would be able to feel Uindok's anger simmering through it in the air. Songas sat on the top of one of the loose crates surrounding the tower.

"Tarias will answer for his crimes in front of the Koroark."

Tarias gulped at the thought of it. He tried to hide the memory of his execution.

"It is an unforgivable act for one to kill an elf from the line of Elreineir, but his circumstance is peculiar. He ought to be given some leniency when he is seeking to right his wrongs."

Uindok grimaced. "Go on, Songas. Let us get to the plan already. I want to see this mongrel hung sooner than later."

Songas looked to Tarias. "Have you found a proper battlefield?"

"Yes. Do you remember where you took me after the Yellow Aucs sewer?"

Songas nodded. "That is a good place. I like that choice."

Uindok crossed his arms. "But what of the explosives?"

"Unfortunately, there is nothing we can truly do about them now. We do not know anything about Nakneir's plan, and with the way he is handling his information, we likely do not have the time to find out. If he is to kill the Koroark, he would seek out his blade first."

Uindok nodded. "You are right. That Nakneir is a strange one. Obsessive, he is. Out of us all, only I am skilled enough to take him on, but even then it would be a hard-won fight. We would need to split him away from his comrades."

Tarias grabbed a loose stick and pointed it at a patch of dry dirt below them. He drew an outline of the city with its Aucs lined out. Afterward, he marked the location of the field outside of the Blue Aucs.

"He and any of his subordinates would likely originate from the Green or the Black, so we will need to monitor any movement south. Songas would be the best to watch—"

Songas extended his hand. "Do not insult Uindok and I, Tarias. Even if you were a true soul seeker, you would only introduce your input upon request. For now, shut your mouth and let us discuss the plan."

Uindok grinned after Songas interrupted Tarias. Uindok's hatred must have been so raw and intense that he could not entertain the thought of acting peacefully with Tarias.

"Despite Tarias stepping out of line, his words were true," Songas said. "I will keep watch and filter out the thoughts of our enemy. Uindok, you will use your elves to set an ambush in the field. Use the far-out brush and any other means to conceal your movements. As for Tarias, Nakneir's dagger is one thing, but the elf who murdered Princess Elreina, heiress to the Realm of Elves and only child of the Koroark, is another. You are going to sit on the southern tip of the Green Aucs. You *will* cause a ruckus and gain attention. Attack some random official and get the attention of another soul seeker. I do not care what you do, for the consequences of us not succeeding in this mission today will mark the end of Teruk."

Tarias nodded. "I can do that."

Songas produced the dagger from under his red jant to hand it to Uindok, and Uindok opened a black box made of stone and placed the blade inside.

"Whatever sensory ability Nakneir or his underlings have to find this blade may as well be mute now. I will try my best to stray the thoughts of his underlings to split them up, but you must bring enough elves with you in case my efforts fail. The safest assumption is that half of them would be confused enough to lose their route, but they will eventually regain their senses before I join you from behind."

Tarias crossed his arms. "The unknown factor is Nakneir's battle capability. I saw nothing in the visions that could hint at what it may be."

"Whatever it is, it will be dealt with upon its discovery. We cannot plan against something we do not know."

"The blade will really be more of a tool to annoy Nakneir, but we cannot assume that it will have so much power over him. He is an obsessive prick, but he is a smart one, too," muttered Uindok.

"Agreed. Realistically, the only bait worth anything is Tarias. We need to plan his route, and then we must plan for a proper day."

"It cannot be anytime soon, not while the cloth festival is going on. There are far too many foreigners and travelers on the roads. Once chaos breaks loose, your mind would be bombarded with their thoughts."

"That means we have the rest of the week to wait. Let us all get our things in order in the meantime. I do not think any of us needs to be reminded to keep our mouths shut and our minds elsewhere."

Uindok and Tarias nodded. Uindok displaced away, leaving Songas and Tarias alone. They entered Songas's chamber.

"The last time you were ordered to stay in one place, you disobeyed."

"I obeyed for many days."

"You still disobeyed, and I found you. I am not ordering you to stay here, but if you want to clear your conscience, you better hope to the Koroark that you have the strength to stay."

Tarias shrugged. "I have no reason to leave."

"Wonderful. Remember, you still need more practice with your visions."

Songas waved Tarias goodbye and displaced. Tarias immediately went for the kneeling mat in the middle of the chamber. He understood quite intimately that the likes of Uindok, Adoneir, Nakneir, and Songas were all at a different, higher, level to himself. He might have been able to handle himself against Nakneir's subordinates, but Nakneir himself? Or even a potential second of his? It would be absurd. He would have to get better. He needed to get better. But how would he?

His eyes locked onto a small wooden ball. A thought sprouted in his mind. He rushed to grab the small ball and looked around for a target. He saw Elreina's ribbon, and there was a small iron hook that protruded from the cellar walls. His hands gently rested the ribbon over the hook. It felt wrong for him to tie it, for he did not want to potentially cause damage to something Songas cared so much about. He stood in the middle of the room, and he focused his throwing hand.

He focused on the thought of what would happen if he threw the ball at the ribbon.

He whipped the wooden ball at the wall, and the drag of it soaring through the cellar air pulled the ribbon down. The green ribbon floated and spun in twirly motions to the cellar ground.

Tarias opened his eyes, and the ribbon still hung on top of the hook. He whipped the ball at the wall, and the same outcome from his visions was produced right in front of him, in *reality*. He squinted at his hands, and he walked over to the wall to place the ribbon back where Songas had left it. He had the ability to see the proper future, and he had the power to do something about his visions. He walked around the cellar while attempting to focus on the outcome of whatever would happen to them if he attempted an action, and every single time, the expected outcome had occurred, again, in *reality*. There was no question in his mind that whatever he could see was near certain to happen, but only if he did not do anything to prevent it.

For every moment he was not sleeping, eating, or drinking, he was training his mind's ability to see the future. His body, at this moment, fell behind his mind in importance. Any time that he previously would have delegated to exercising his body now went toward exercising his ability to think.

After countless visions, Tarias noticed his arms. He did not feel tired. His visions did not drain him the way displacement had. He smiled, and for the rest of his conscious hours that day, he continued to train.

CHAPTER 22

The Palace of Aigerua was down the road, and blue banners were behind Tarias. He walked down the center of the road, to the dismay of the Midlandesq that walked against him. Their glares were plentiful and severe, and soon enough, an elf with a tall black hat with green and gold decoration—a magistrate—strutted forward. He was flanked by two armored elves in green jants and black lamellar. The crowd began to disperse at this moment by the wag of his finger.

"You there! You imbecile! What gives you the thought that you may walk down the center?"

"It is a road, is it not for walking?" asked Tarias.

Tarias was dressed in an old gray robe with no shoes on his feet. Everyone around him wore some form of sandal or boot while wearing the latest fashion of jant in the most pungent of colors. The elf came forward and pushed him to the side.

"Get! Go back to the edge, where you belong!"

Tarias stumbled and fell. He feigned a look of shock while he pulled himself to his feet. He brushed the dirt off of his robes and shook his head. His fist soon landed on the cheek of the magistrate. The guards immediately pulled their bludgeons from their side. One swung forward, and Tarias displaced out of the way. The magistrate gasped and wagged his finger, yelling for his guards to apprehend Tarias, but Tarias ran. Whistling roared in the streets, but the whistling soon turned into alarm bells. The pedestrians vacated the streets, and azkozal-mounted elves pursued Tarias. Tarias, still on his feet, could not outrun them, so once the first swing of their curved swords met him, he displaced onto the back of the elf riding an azkozal and pulled him from the bird.

Tarias did not often ride, but he was no stranger to it. He slapped the reins, and the azkozal went into a sprint.

Slow down, Tarias heard in his mind.

He reared the azkozal a bit, and immediately a volley of arrows ripped passed his face from the alley at his side. He heard cursing, and he sent the bird once more into a sprint. By this time, all the elves had run into the adjacent buildings. He could feel them peering through the windows. He could sense their awe, and their roars for his capture encouraged his pursuers to chase him with an ever-growing fervor.

Abandon the bird!

Tarias did not hesitate to leap off the azkozal. Its anisodactyl feet were pierced by a field of fell caltrops. His pursuers kept their sprint. Their azkozals met a similar fate. They were shot off their mounts into the caltrops below. Tarias smiled at his evasion, but a figure manifested before him. It was a figure born from black dust, but it was not Nakneir. It was a Sealandesq elf with a blade in hand. He wore black, and his eyes drooped with disgust.

"Our lowly kind always seems to step out of line," said the elf, producing a dagger from each sleeve.

Tarias grinned. "Very much so. Let Nakneir know I have his blade, and that I am the elf who has slain his son."

The elf's eyes shot wide. He lunged for Tarias, but Tarias anticipated it and skipped to the side. He ran down the alleyway for the Blue Aucs. Not but a few moments later, the repetitive ringing pattern of the alarm bells changed to a more staggered period. It kept the same pattern until Tarias had shifted in direction, and soon the pattern had changed. It had to have been deliberate, so Tarias shifted south once more, and the first staggered pattern had returned. *They were following his movements*, he thought, and this filled Tarias with joy.

He made it to the Blue Aucs. The Sealandesq elves took refuge only when Tarias had finally arrived. They were curious. They undoubtedly wished to see what elf had the gall to strike a Green Aucs magistrate. The energy of the cheering seemed to have altered. Instead of rooting for the guards to apprehend Tarias, they cheered for him to get away. Tarias had never noticed Sealandesq ever act against the Midlandesq, and this jumbled his thoughts for a moment.

Continue on, Tarias!

Songas ripped him out of his tangential thoughts and back to the firm reality he was in. *He had to get to the wall.* The Blue Aucs was vast. It was so vast that Tarias was beginning to grow tired, but displacing at this moment would certainly mean his death. If he were to displace outside the wall, his body would not have the ability to move; if he displaced even further, his body likely would not be able to recover. He would fade into nothingness.

The distance to the wall was a third of the distance to cross from one side of Aigerua to the other. Tarias would have to find another azkozal or some other way to get to the edge of the city. Taking the sewers was out of the question, as he could not afford to lose his tail. He continued to run. If Songas had not been there to aid him, Tarias would have surely been caught. The guards would have reached him by now, or they would have been *present*, but there were no guards in the streets. The Blue Aucs was empty.

As Tarias gained more distance away from the Green Aucs, the alarm bells faded. With the cacophony gone, it was like he was taking a quiet run in the early morning, but the sun was halfway through the sky. Any azkozals that were on the road were left hitched by the watering streams that paralleled them. He untied one of their reins and hopped on, taking the road toward the wall.

He was halfway through the Blue Aucs when the alarm bells returned. They made the same pattern as when he was going south in the Green. His gaze wandered around to the tops of the buildings. Elf-sized clouds of black mist appeared on top of them. He tried to count them all, but there were far too many. *Why, no,* how *were there so many?* Were soul seekers not rare all of a sudden? They finally took form. There was one on every rooftop. Dozens of soul seekers all dressed in black jants and armed with bows aimed their arrows for Tarias. A barrage of arrows pierced into the brick roads.

He sent the bird into a zigzag sprint to the wall, but an arrow pierced the bum of the bird. Thankfully, this sent the azkozal into an even faster, yet panicked, sprint. The gates were growing closer. The wall was about a hundred heads away, and he was soon to it.

A spear pierced through the bird. It stuck so deep it cut the side of Tarias's thigh. He was bucked off the bird, and his body flew through the air; but instead of landing on the brick road, he landed on the grass outside of the Aigeruan walls. He huffed for air. The fatigue set in, but he could not lay there and let himself get captured. He lifted himself and rushed for the field. His gait was uneven because of the cut. His left leg dragged behind him while his right pulled him forward with desperation. He heard yelling. He looked behind them, the soul seekers were pursuing him. They displaced once more, and they had their bows already aimed.

Fuck, he thought.

Run, Tarias!

Tarias tried to forget about his injury, and he *ran*. Arrows pelted around him again. His heart raced faster than his legs, and he desperately attempted to speed up. He attempted to zig-zag, but the elves were not aiming for *him*, they were aiming all around him. An arrow hissed passed his head, loudly enough for him to reach and see if the arrowhead had taken his ear with it. Thankfully, when Tarias reached to see his hand, it was neither crimson nor wet.

His foot caught itself in a mole hole. He fell face-first to the dirt ground. The arrows were surely soon to pelt him, so he rolled onto his back to accept his fate. He attempted to focus on the arrows. Maybe he could prevent his death. He blinked, but he was not dead. He had not been saved by Songas, Uindok, or even one of his elves. There were not even arrows coming to kill him. There Nakneir stood, standing over the fallen soul seeker.

At first, he held a grin of manic malice, but soon, tears ran from his eyes. However, he did not sulk. He had a look of contempt carved into his face.

"You ruined it all. You killed my son. You ruined it all!"

He knelt on top of Tarias. The back of his hand struck Tarias's cheek.

"I raised him. I spent so many fucking days of my life carving him into a proper heir, and you just go and kill him? You are a thorn in my side. A splinter in my finger. Where is my blade? I know you have it. You deserve to be killed by it. I wish to experience your deserved death every day for as long as I reign."

Tarias tilted his head. "What? You aren't the Koroark."

Nakneir snarled his lip. "You are a slave to me. You are a lowly Sealandesq pawn, a defective *tool*. What do you know of the Koroark? You thought you were taking orders from that false monarch, but you were taking them from *me*. You are nothing without me. I have made you into what you are today, and you threw it out because your stupid little heart could not tolerate *doing what needed to be done*. You are not a soul seeker, and you never have been. You wanted purpose in life. I had Adoneir give you that purpose, yet you threw it out because you are a coward. A scared little orphan. You were on the streets because no one wanted you, and now I see why. You are *useless*."

By now, Nakneir's army had marched over. They stood at the ready around the tyrant, but they were met with a swift kick to their liege's stomach. It was an elf dressed in a blue war-jant. He wore lamellar that covered his torso and his shoulders. His war-jant was thick, and its sleeves covered all the way down to his wrists. Nakneir heaved, for the armored metal shin of the elf had surely struck him hard. The elf displaced again, but this time he was behind Nakneir, his fist already being sent to the back of his crown. Nakneir's subordinates rushed forward, and to their surprise, a dozen elves, also dressed in blue, began to strike them from behind. Half defended, and the other half continued to rush to the aid of their lord. Even with being caught by surprise, the ambushers were far too outnumbered to be effective, so the elves in black jants rushed in with confidence. The elves in blue did not falter, and they fought like the numbers of the enemy were of no consequence. One by one, Nakneir's elves were cut down; however, Uindok's elves grew tired and had to displace more frequently to keep up with the enemy.

Uindok was focused on Nakneir. His armored fists battered the false emperor with primal fury, but he was not tense. There was a strange looseness beneath all that armor. He looked more like an armored dancer than an armored brute. Tarias had never seen someone displace with so much elegance or with such little exertion. Maybe this was what Songas had meant when he said Uindok did not tire.

Even though Uindok moved so effortlessly, Nakneir seemed like he was keeping up. Uindok was still slightly faster than the false Koroark, but Nakneir took each hit and continued without noticeable injury. Nakneir displaced far away with frustration, raised his fist into the air, and *squeezed.* His army was displaced, and his elves now surrounded the Blue Esku's fatigued soul seekers. They had spears in their hands, and they thrust forward with finality. A third of his elves fell to the ground, their torsos looking like honeycomb, and the rest displaced. Uindok turned his head and stared at the sight. He turned back with a clenched fist that burned with hatred. He squeezed his hand with such pressure that it could have produced heat, and he displaced to Nakneir, throwing punch after punch.

Nakneir produced a mace out of thin air and swung it into the Blue Esku's side, leaving a noticeable dent in the plates that composed his lamellar coat. He stumbled and displaced away to recoup from his injury. It must have been a clean hit, because he took a good amount of time to hold his side and get air back into his lungs. Tarias felt the need to help, so he climbed up to his feet and shambled forward. Nakneir pointed at him and laughed.

"You are a joke! Look at you trying to come toward me. It is embarrassing. You are nowhere near the level of that elf, and you think you can help him? You can barely even move, you squashed roach."

Tarias's eyes wandered as he attempted to focus on what was around him. The only visions he saw led to his defeat. Nakneir had a wide grin on his face.

"Oh! Adoneir was right. You can see the future, you can! How terrible that such a wonderful gift was wasted on such a pitiful creature. That blade is near, I know it. I can feel it. I have sensed it within your mind. I will have my elves dig it up for me."

Nakneir looked down.

"Looks like it is beneath my feet. I am going to kill you with it to discover what visions you have seen."

Tarias continued to stumble forward. The elf that he had seen in the alleyway while on his pursuit displaced in front of him, a blade in each hand. He grinned from ear to ear. Tarias looked around. Soul seekers dressed in black jants displaced around them, further outnumbering the Blues.

"Keep that one alive while I fetch my dagger."

Nakneir started to dig with his hands. The soul seeker walked forward and sheathed his blades to free his hands and apprehend Tarias. Tarias readied his fists, but truly, he saw no future where he would win.

Suddenly, one of the elves screamed. He *howled*. The elf rushed his hand to his heart, tears draining from his eyes. The sounds of torment erupted all around Tarias. Nakneir lifted his head and placed his hand on his forehead, much like how one would with a sudden migraine. Tarias spun around. All the elves in black were also suffering, much like how the soul seeker had. They collapsed to the ground in anguish. Their screams were horrific. The way they writhed reminded Tarias of his many nights of guilt. He remembered the panic he felt.

Before him, there was a field of elves suffering from his thoughts.

An elf dressed in red came walking from the direction of Aigerua. He was angry. Songas's free spirit was nowhere to be found. It was replaced by eyes filled with clear direction. Laughter sounded behind Tarias.

"That makes sense! You are the reason why my elves were split up in Aigerua. You sent them astray! I should have expected to see you in the fray. You always have been like a pesky rash to me, with how you made things more difficult than they should have been. Are you happy now? Are you happy that your childhood friend is dead? Or she who you loved, Elreina, are you happy that she is dead, too? This elf before you—Tarias, was it? He too will be dead. The Yellow Aucs, the Blue, and the Red. All shall be gone. Everything you have ever loved will be gone, you sympathizer. You are one of us, but you care only for *roaches* and *foreigners.*"

Nakneir struck his hand into the ground and pulled the dagger from it. He pointed it forward.

"Remember that, Songas! Ferment that fact in your heart, and know it before I kill you!"

Songas walked forward with a blade in hand. He walked past the dozens of fallen soldiers, sometimes having to take a long stride over a pile of dejected elves. He did not speak to Nakneir, simply staring with a tired expression, ready to end the battle. With haste, Nakneir appeared in front of Songas and stabbed his blade forward. Songas had already dodged the thrust before Nakneir even appeared. He moved before Nakneir even attacked. Nakneir took a step back and chuckled.

"Ha! You are reading my thoughts."

Nakneir raised his palm, and a black stone mask formed in his hands. He placed it on his face and choked his dagger's hilt.

"No more of this stupid back and forth!"

He lunged forward at Songas, and this time, Songas took a noticeably longer period of time to respond. His evasions were far less elegant, and he was now taking hits from the tyrant. An unarmored elf in a war-jant appeared behind

Nakneir and slammed his fist into the side of his lower back. Nakneir's back arched and he lost his balance. The Red and Blue Esku took turns kicking the Black Esku while he was down. He disappeared, and a wooden wagon manifested above the two Eskus, plummeting towards them. Uindok grabbed Songas and displaced the both of them about a dozen leg-lengths away from where they stood. Nakneir appeared behind Uindok, kicked the back of his knee in, and followed with an elbow to the back of his head. The Blue Esku flopped dazedly down to the grassy field. Songas tackled Nakneir, and the two devolved into a state of wrestling with each other on the ground.

Tarias shook his head. He squeezed his hands into fists, angry at the fact that he stood so idly by while Songas and Uindok fought Nakneir. He looked around. The screaming elf had disappeared, and a blade of one of the fallen soldiers rested on the ground. He grabbed it and began to walk determinedly toward the tyrant.

He stopped. What was he thinking? He could not compete with the twin of the Koroark. What skill did he have that could set him equal to him? He could not displace with such efficiency as Uindok, Nakneir, or even Songas. Moving himself but a few feet left him huffing for air. He focused on the tyrant. He stared him down, wondering what might happen.

Songas, Tarias thought.

Songas turned his head to face Tarias with a questioning glare.

Be aware of my thoughts.

Tarias focused his gaze on Nakneir. He thought of his actions and what they might do. He knelt and let the visions come to him. Songas reacted as fast as he had before Nakneir put on the mask. Tarias heard a grunt in the distance. Nakneir must have been struck. This put a smile on his face.

His neck felt like it was being crushed. Nakneir's hand clasped tight around it like a vice.

"You are almost too annoying to let live. I have to quit being so picky and just kill you already."

Nakneir whipped his dagger out and pulled it back. He struck forward, delving deep into its victim's flesh. Uindok's body leaned forward onto Tarias with Nakneir's blade piercing through his torso. Nakneir pushed the Blue Esku's body off of his blade, and once it fell down, Tarias punched the tyrant square in the jaw. Nakneir fell backward, and Tarias ripped the mask off of him and threw it behind him. The Black Esku had a confused look on his face like he could not comprehend why Uindok would sacrifice himself for Tarias. After sending elbow after elbow down into the face of the tyrant, Tarias stripped the dagger from his hands. Nakneir displaced to his wobbly feet, ready to fight. Songas, now behind the Black Esku, wrapped his arm around his neck and *squeezed*. Tarias, with Nakneir's blade in his hand, stabbed the false Koroark repeatedly until his weakened body went limp.

Songas released the strangle, and Nakneir fell to his knees. He tried to laugh, but he reached for his torso in pain once it set in.

"You idiots. You have won this battle, but I've won another. We *will* be rid of you parasitic ordinaries."

CHAPTER 23

"Uindok!" Songas rushed to the side of the Esku.

He felt around for a pulse. Uindok's chest still rose, so Songas looked to call for the Blue Esku's elves. But before he could even muster a breath, an elf in a blue jant was already at his side. About a moment later, the rest of them had displaced there.

"We will handle our master. He would want you to end this," said one of the soul seekers.

Songas nodded to him. He grabbed Tarias and pointed at Nakneir.

"Focus! Focus on the future now! Look to the city and figure out what he meant!"

Tarias tried, but he was blind. He saw nothing. There was absolutely nothing to be seen, Nakneir was already dead. There was no future to be had from him. *He was gone.*

"Try harder, Tarias! There must be something. There *has* to be something."

Songas's mannerisms were out of the ordinary. Tarias could feel his anxiety, and it reminded him much of his own. What had Nakneir meant when he said he won a battle? What battle would he have won?

The explosives were still out there, Tarias realized. And where was the soul seeker in black who bore two blades? He thought back. What could be happening? Tarias turned his head to the soul seekers in blue.

"Are you going to displace him back to Aigerua?"

They nodded.

"Take me and Songas with you. It is imperative."

Songas grabbed Tarias. "What did you see? I did not see it."

"I saw nothing; it is a hunch. I believe Nakneir planned to blow up the Red, Blue, and Yellow Aucs."

The blue soul seekers all shot stares at one another.

"We will have to displace to the Green, then."

Songas nodded his head. They all grabbed one another in some manner, and soon they all stood in the streets of the Green Aucs. They were at the Statue of Ee'nak. Tarias stared straight for the Yellow, focusing forward.

He saw dozens of explosions spread around one by one all over the district. It was not the Yellow Aucs alone, for south in the Blue and west in the Red also blew up into a myriad of fireballs.

Tarias opened his eyes to Songas staring at him with a dropped jaw.

"Where do you suspect the explosives to be?"

Tarias furrowed his brow, deep in thought. He thought back to the beginning. *Where would they put the explosives?* The thought then hit him.

"Songas, you said the Yellow Esku was busy with his own matters in the Yellow Aucs. What were the matters?"

Songas looked down. "I should not be saying it. I am bound by oath, but I feel this moment is an exception I may make. There were several executions of Sealandesq elves of no relation. Soon, there were mobs of Sealandesq elves looking for justice, and violence broke out between Sealandesq and Midlandesq elves. He was investigating their origin."

Songas was hit with a realization.

"The sewers. Adoneir was acting in the sewers, so Nakneir must have ordered it."

"There have been random intrusions into the Blue Aucs sewers recently," said one of the elves in blue.

Songas looked down. "I have heard a similar story throughout the Red. I will head there now. Whoever can head for the Blue, please do so. As for the Yellow, Tarias, head for their sewers—you know where they have been. The Koroark must be notified of this. We simply do not have enough elves to combat them on our own."

One of Uindok's soul seekers stepped forward. "I will inform the Koroark. Let us hope the Greens are quick to come to our aid."

"If you may, urge the Koroark to send a few of the Gilded. We will need the most effective to minimize the damage. We must hurry! Take an azkozal and ride!"

The soul seeker nodded his head and displaced. They all rushed to their respective destinations. Tarias let his mind forget about his pesky leg and rushed for the nearest hitched azkozal. He hopped on top and sent it into a sprint for the Yellow. The ride felt far too long for the distance he was making. He had to be there *now*. There was no time to waste. His vision became a tunnel heading directly for the Yellow.

In no time, he was at the sewer he had been ambushed in not too long ago. He hopped off the azkozal and stood at the edge. The sewer lid was open, and the flashing of torchlight faintly emanated from within. He grabbed a nearby rock and climbed down into the sewer once more. Constant chattering sounded from within. Mushy footsteps continuously echoed from inside the sewers. Tarias's feet landed on the sewer floor. Boxes, ones that were not present before, were placed after every twelfth leg in the sewer tunnels. They were about two hands tall and two hands wide. Tarias grabbed one of them. He opened the top, and inside there was a silvery white powder within that held its own glow.

"Who are you?" inquired an unknown voice.

Without thinking, Tarias shot forward and attacked the elf. He punched him in the face and shoved him into the wall. The elf dropped his weapon, and his eyes darted around with fear. Tarias looked him up and down. He wore a black jant, and he was a Midlandesq elf. He turned his head around, and in the middle of the sewer, there were three dead elves all wearing yellow.

"I am Tarias."

He punched the elf, sending him to the ground. He grabbed the blade and pierced his heart. Voices were heard around the corner, and they ran to Tarias. Tarias readied his blade forward.

"It's that elf! The one who punched the magistrate!"

Those words were that elf's last. Tarias threw the blade, and it pierced the elf in the chest. He ran forward to meet them in combat. They lunged with their blades, but they were no match for the soul seeker. Tarias *saw* their next move, and he spun around their attacks with a similar elegance as Songas had. With but a few strokes of his hand, they all lay bloody and dying in the sewer.

There was no line to the explosives. They were simply going to be set off from each other. The sewers were sparsely populated, and whoever was still present seemed to be evacuating. Tarias rushed forward and focused.

A burning white fireball came in front of him, incinerating him.

Tarias opened his eyes. He knew he was going in the right direction, so he ran forward. Whenever he met a junction where the path split, he *focused*. He saw his own death, his own incineration, several times before making it to a chamber where a countless number of explosives were stored. The soul seeker who was dressed in black stood in the center of them. He held a silvery glowing metal in his hand, and he stepped back to toss it into the explosives.

"Stop!" yelled Tarias.

He turned back, and Tarias threw a stone at him. He ducked down, attempting to save the metal from its fall.

"You idiot! You almost killed the both of us with your recklessness." He gently placed the metal ingot down.

"I know. The powder that fills those explosives is the same as that ingot."

"I thought you would want to save—"

Tarias displaced next to the soul seeker. He did not manifest quickly enough, and the soul seeker reacted, but Tarias already *saw* the attack. Tarias ducked down and swept the soul seeker off of his feet. He reached for a blade, but Tarias stomped on his hand, forcing him to drop it to the ground. He secured the blade in his own hands, and the soul seeker rolled on his side and back to his feet. He pulled the other blade from his waist, and the two pointed their blades at one another.

"Get out of here," said the elf. "You have already lost. I am but one of a few. Do not think that taking me out will secure a victory. We just need one to explode, and you rats will be *dead*."

Tarias stood there and said nothing. This angered the elf in black. He rattled his blade forward.

"Are you not going to advance? What type of soul seeker are you?"

Tarias did not move.

"ATTACK ME!"

"I refuse."

Tarias held the blade forward, and the soul seeker stared at Tarias with a dumbfounded expression.

"Why?" asked the soul seeker.

"Because if I move from here, you will win. You need this ingot to set off the explosives."

"I can remove you from there."

"No, you cannot. You know I can see the future, and there is no future where you secure this from me. If you displace here, you will be cut down. And if I am wrong, then you will not have enough energy to vacate from the immediate explosion. I have *seen it*. There is no event that you succeed other than the one I freely leave this spot, so I shall stand here."

The elf grimaced. He gritted his teeth, and his head wandered with frustration. He returned his gaze to Tarias, snarling.

"I suppose you are right, but do know that you have still lost."

The elf displaced away out of the chamber. Tarias sat down cross-legged and waited. In truth, he saw numerous visions where he had died in that tunnel. He saw visions where, undoubtedly, the others had failed to stop Nakneir's elves, but he still chose to stay. If he were to die in those tunnels, so be it. He would have deserved it for all his past actions. It would have been wrong for him to complain and worry. He deserved death, so he waited in that tunnel so that others could live.

"You. Step away from that ingot."

It was an elf in gilded armor. He walked forward with his hand resting on his longblade. Tarias nodded and got to his feet, away from the piece of silvery metal. The Gilded grabbed the ingot and handed it to another elf, one who was dressed in a green jant. That elf displaced, leaving Tarias in the room with the Gilded.

"State your name and why you are here."

"I am Tarias, and I prevented the detonation of these explosives."

The elf squinted his eyes. "Come here. You are being apprehended. I will bring you before the Koroark, and his divine will shall determine if your words are true."

Tarias walked forward. He held his wrists out to the Gilded, his chin tucked down. The Gilded pulled shackles from his side and bound Tarias's wrists. A group of other elves dressed in green came from the tunnel, and he ordered them to remove the explosives from the sewers. They nodded and ran off. He placed his hand on Tarias's shoulder, and he displaced to the outside of the Palace of Aigerua.

Songas stood there, too. His wrists were also bound, and his body was covered in red, but it was not the same red from his jant. Another elf in gilded armor stood next to him, and a few more Gilded stood to Tarias's right. They had a few of Uindok's Blues apprehended and bound.

Tarias looked to Songas. "Did you prevent them from being detonated?"

Songas smiled and nodded. Tarias looked to his right, and the Blues did the same. The Gilded that bounded Tarias stepped forward and cleared his throat.

"You all have been apprehended because of the nature of this event. You all shall be brought before the Koroark to suffer his judgment. I truly do wish for this nightmare to be over, and I pray that none of you hold evil in your hearts."

The Gilded pointed his open palm to the Palace of Aigerua.

CHAPTER 24

Tarias felt fear. He was disgusted with himself. He felt the same feeling he had after he killed Elreina. He saw the visions of all his past doings rush to his mind, but at the same time, he felt it to be an honor he could not flee from. It was an unreal feeling walking through the gates of the Palace of Aigerua, for he was not in disguise. Tarias had come to the Palace in the same gray garb he wore every day.

Tarias, still bound by chains, had the sharp point of a Gilded's spear urging him forward. Songas walked with him to his left, and he was bound as well. To Tarias's right, Uindok's soul seekers were urged by the Gilded's spears, too. They marched for the Palace while the green shrubbery blew in the crisp midday air.

They had succeeded at stopping Nakneir, but Tarias was still filled with sorrow. He thought of the Koroark who was now left with no living family members. Surely, Tarias would die that day, like the vision he had seen before.

They had reached the steps of the Palace itself, and they climbed the many steps up to the open Palace doors. They walked through the divine halls and entered the throne room. The Koroark, in all of his greatness, knelt on the disk on top of the grassy mound. His skin glowed in the same patterns Tarias had seen before, and in each corner of the room, there was a Gilded. In between the Gilded, there were elves dressed in green jants and lamellar. Tarias, Songas, and Uindok's elves were brought before the kneeling god. They were forced to their knees.

The Koroark stood up. He walked down from the disk. He walked with a grace Tarias had not even seen from the most conscious of elves. He was efficient in every movement. His feet seemed to perfectly place themselves down on the mound, like he had walked that same path for centuries. He stood in the middle between all of the soul seekers, and his burning gaze looked over all of them. He prepared to speak.

"Gilded, vacate. None of these elves wish to harm me, and I wish to be alone with them."

The Gilded were taken aback, but they did not even seem for a second to question their god. They, as well as the elves in green, vacated the room. The Koroark still glowed, but his light was now dimming. Tarias got a look into his eyes. They burned with power. This elf, this *deity*, was *raw power*. His blazing gaze burned deep into Tarias.

"You are the most peculiar."

Tarias's eyes darted back and forth, looking for words to say, but he could not form them in his mind. He felt a palm rest on his head.

"Rise."

Tarias hastily rose. He did not want to waste the time of his god.

"For most of your life, you have acted against me. You have killed people who have served me. You have slaughtered innocents. You have gone directly against me."

Songas shuddered with fear. Tarias had never seen him so scared, but he realized that Songas was feeling *Tarias's* fear. Tarias's heart felt like it was dissipating into his limbs. His entire body was beating with fear. He did not even want to defend himself. He *deserved* his fate. He deserved, right then and there, to die.

"You have killed my nephew, killed my brother, and you have killed my heir, my beloved daughter. You have committed sins that would warrant your torture. You have done things so severe that no elf has done before. You have killed numerous members of the royal line of Elreineir. A crime of that severity ought to destine you to a fate worse than a quick execution."

Tarias readied his neck. He ought to die.

"And you, Songas, my most trusted—and you know that I do not say that with a loose tongue—have aided this elf. You have helped him kill my nephew and brother. And upon learning that he had killed my daughter, you did not stop him. You let him live. You, too, rise."

Songas rose, and he kept his head down. He must have felt that he did not deserve to gaze at the Koroark.

"You two know the severity of your actions."

He swiped his hand through the air, and the soul seeker's shackles dissipated into a silvery white mist. Tarias spun his head around in shock. Why had he unbound them?

"The rest of you rise as well."

The Blues did as the Koroark asked.

"You have committed no crime, Songas. You are cursed with compassion. This elf that you have aided before me felt true guilt in his actions, and he truly believed that he was devoted to me. The true criminal lay dead outside Aigerua. My own power-hungry twin brother had turned my nephew against me, and he corrupted this poor, gifted soul. I am in a strange position. How can I allow the elf who has killed my family, despite my family's transgressions, to live? And how am I to allow my subordinate to continue on as though he had not helped him?"

Songas still shuddered with fear.

"You two are far too valuable to me to kill."

All the soul seekers' heads shot up.

"I, like Tarias, can see the future, but with more clarity. You all must live. You all have a role to play. What exactly that is I will not disclose, but to kill any one of you would bring calamity. But I cannot let you stay, either."

His eyes shifted to Songas and Tarias.

"From now on, the Gilded will take over the Eskus' roles. I will be more active. I went against the ancestors by trusting my brother. Perhaps it was a mortal hope for my family to be whole, but I know now that it was foolish. I brought this trouble upon myself. Songas, you are banished from Aigerua."

Songas raised his head with awe. He did not question. He nodded his head and accepted his fate.

"You will bring Tarias under your wing. I know you dislike taking soul seekers, but this is a divine order. You are to make him a proper soul seeker. He will play the most important role of all."

"Where will we go?"

"You are to collect your belongings and head to Eith Island. Their independence is the only reason we are unable to retake the Sealands, so you are to head the espionage and secure what rightfully is ours."

Songas nodded. The Koroark turned his head to Tarias.

"Begone."

In a flash of blinding white light, Songas and Tarias stood outside the Palace of Aigerua. Songas looked different. He was deep in thought.

"Come, Tarias."

"What is it, Songas?"

"We are going back to my chamber. I am going to collect what belongings I wish to bring with us to Eith. We must be gone by dusk, as is the nature of our banishment."

They walked down the winding streets of Aigerua. They walked down the center, and all of the commoners stared at the bloodied elf. They got out of his way. They were intimidated by him, and their fear made Songas's face twitch. It grew so severe that they visited a bathhouse on the way. They figured they ought to wash the muck and blood off of themselves so that they might not offend the streetwalkers. By the time they were done washing away their grime, the sun was low in the sky. They dried themselves off and came out of the baths clean.

Tarias stopped. "I wish to visit somewhere one last time before I go."

Songas turned his head to Tarias. "Go."

Tarias ran off. He made several turns, but he finally made it to his destination. It was the home that had been rewarded to him by Adoneir, its door still open wide. He walked in and went to his room. Again, nothing but the mirror was in the room, but that did not matter. He wanted the mirror.

He walked out of the house with the mirror tucked under his arm. The elves in the street were a bit annoyed with the space he was taking up, but Tarias let himself be oblivious to their glares. He wanted to give his tired mind a rest. He stared at the pruned trees that lined the streets. They were always what he enjoyed the most about the roads. Their always-green leaves gave them a calm aura, something the people of Aigerua needed.

He had reached the Red Aucs. Songas must have already climbed down the tower. He opened the door and placed the mirror inside. Afterward, he opened the trap door and climbed down into the chamber. Songas was packing. He was in no rush to leave. He dragged his feet along the chamber floors like a sad puppy. He stood with Elreina's ribbon in hand. His eyes looked deep into it like he was reading its past.

He looked to Tarias.

"Where did you go?"

"I went to retrieve something."

Songas looked off into space with a blank stare. "You retrieved something? That mirror. You retrieved the *mirror?* Why?"

"It is a reminder of all the bad things I have done. I must remember so that I may properly atone. I feel that I have not yet done so."

"You saved the city, Tarias. You prevented the deaths of countless elves. In a way, despite the pain you have caused numerous innocents, you have saved countless more. That should be something to relieve some pain from your aching heart."

"I suppose, but I do not think I have done enough."

"You never will think you have done enough."

Songas continued to pack his things. Tarias looked over to a shelf on the wall. It was the shelf that the handle of Adoavi had rested on top of. Tarias walked over to it and placed it into his hands.

"I suppose now is as good a time as any. You have nothing to pack, and we cannot go until I am finished. You may read the blade, Tarias."

Tarias nodded, and he focused on the blade of Adoavi.